"I'm not used to being scared," she said.

"A lot of people are."

"But I'm not. Do you think I'm overreacting?"

"Having a person you're meeting shot before your eyes is still not real common in most sections of L.A. It'd make me jittery, too."

The shot tore through her and landed in the wall a few inches from my ear. I crawled to the girl. She was hit in the shoulder; no more than a scratch, really. I said a few comforting things I remembered from a recent *Starsky and Hutch*. Shootings were a definite strain on me.

CARPENTER, DETECTIVE

HAMILTON T. CAINE

CHARTER
NEW YORK

A DIVISION OF CHARTER COMMUNICATIONS INC.
A GROSSET & DUNLAP COMPANY

CARPENTER, DETECTIVE
Copyright © 1980 by Stephen Smoke

A Charter Original.

First Charter Printing January 1981
Published simultaneously in Canada
Manufactured in the United States of America

2 4 6 8 0 9 7 5 3 1

TO SANDY

- - - - - - -

AND A SPECIAL THANKS TO PAUL BISHOP

It was an autumn night. An autumn night in Los Angeles. That is to say, you couldn't tell it from any other night of the year. Mirabelle's was going strong for a Wednesday and Spike the bartender—I still have faith that someday I'll meet a bartender with a real name—was telling me how the British make a Pimm's. The conversation finally got a little too boring for us both . . . how much can anyone say about how to make a drink with only two ingredients? I was seriously considering stuffed mushrooms at Cyrano when a brunette who looked like she had something serious on her mind walked in, past me, and over to Spike. She called him "Buddy," but she did it nice. He seemed to respond better to her, at least with more enthusiasm, than he did to me, and we were close. I figured I'd still call him Spike. I think it was her legs, not her ease with names, that impressed him the most. It was what impressed *me* the most. Her body was a museum full of pieces of art. But the closer I looked, the more the museum started to look like a playground. She wore a black dress with a slit up one side; no stockings. I wondered what else she wasn't wearing.

Then I heard her say, "I'm looking for Ace Carpenter."

I always hated the name Ace. It wasn't like my parents gave it to me or anything, but it was a handle that

1

stuck no matter how many times I tried to break it off. We had a bad relationship, my name and I.

"Buddy" looked a little less enthusiastic after she said my name.

"That's him," he said, pointing to me. Actually he didn't point. I was so close that if he had pointed he would have stuck his finger up my nose. He just tilted his head in my direction.

She took aim on me and shot a near-fatal glance my way. I had the feeling she had looked at other men that way and knew what it did to them. I came to as fast as I could.

"So you're a detective?" she said.

A lot of funny things came to mind, but I decided to save them for a more intimate time.

"Yeah. What can I do for you?"

"My name is Kathy St. John," she began. "A friend of mine, Penny Silverstein, gave me your number. And your answering service told me I could find you here."

Penny Silverstein. A name from my past. A few nights in the sack and—in spite of them—we became, if not close, at least perennial friends. She occasionally threw some business my way and I appreciated it. I tried to reciprocate. She was a masseuse/hooker . . . either one, depending on how close it was to rent time and how tight it was—her financial squeeze, that is.

"She said you helped her find her lost kittens."

"Yeah, well . . ." I brushed off the comment, not because I was embarrassed, but because I didn't want to dwell on it. A potential client might overhear us and probably wouldn't be overly impressed by my ability to find lost animals.

"Could we talk in private?" she asked.

"Sure," I said, and ushered her to the darkest corner I could find.

"I think I need some protection," she said after we were seated.

"From whom?"

"I'm not certain," she replied, crossing her legs so that the slit opened and exposed a beautiful tanned thigh. "You know about the shooting at the Old World Restaurant this afternoon?"

"Just a stone's throw away. Sure, I heard about it."

The evening news had been full of the stuff. Earlier in the afternoon some guy with a beard had been shot in front of the restaurant, apparently by someone with a rifle from across the street. The guy with the beard had been wounded, but was able to get away. Neither the wounded man nor the assailant had been apprehended.

"Well, last night a man called me and asked me to meet him today for lunch at the Old World. He said I would recognize him because he would have a beard and be wearing a beige sweater. I arrived at the restaurant at 1:45 P.M., just fifteen minutes before our proposed meeting time. At exactly 2:00 this guy with a beard and a beige sweater came strolling up the sidewalk to the restaurant and boom! he got shot."

I rolled what was left of my Pimm's around a few times in my glass and finally said, "Did you stay long after that?"

"About another half hour. And no one else with a beard and a beige sweater showed up."

"What made you make a date with a man you'd never met before?"

She paused and looked away. She uncrossed her legs. Now I was sorry I'd asked the question. She was thinking.

"He was a friend of Penny's. He said so, and I checked with Penny to make sure after he called."

To me, that didn't exactly equal a four-star rating, but I didn't push it. I'd ask Penny myself. Kathy had told me all she planned to tell me.

"So what exactly do you want me to do?"

"I'm scared. Penny is my best friend and she says

you're a good guy, besides being the closest thing to a detective either of us knows."

Somehow that didn't sound too complimentary.

"So, if you would see me home tonight, check out the closets, you know, I'd feel a lot safer. After a couple days of protection, I'm sure I'll feel a lot better about things. But right now I need someone to check out my apartment. I haven't been back there since the shooting this afternoon."

The assignment sounded great to me. I paid my tab and followed her over to her place.

She lived on Gardner, just above Hollywood Boulevard, in a little apartment with a view and a cat named Blacky. The cat was black. I was beginning to see the way she figured things. She was a simple girl. And I liked simple girls; especially ones with great legs.

I did a thorough check of her apartment and it turned up nothing except her spirits, which were now at the highest level of the evening.

She came into the bedroom, the last room to be checked, and gave me a warm smile. Ever since I'd first laid eyes on Kathy I'd hoped I'd end up in her bedroom and that she'd be smiling at me.

She walked across the room toward me. God, she walked great.

"Like a drink?"

"Sure," I said. "Whatcha got?"

"Beer, wine, orange and apple juice."

"I'll take a beer."

I sat down in a bean-bag chair opposite the foot of her bed and she went to get me a beer.

When Kathy returned she said, "Here you are," and handed me a dark brew. She sat down on her bed facing me. She'd brought herself a glass of orange juice.

"I'm not used to being scared," she said.

"A lot of people are."

"But I'm not. Do you think I'm overreacting?"

"Having a person you're meeting shot before your eyes is still not real common in most sections of L.A. It'd make me jittery, too."

"It's not like in the movies. I mean the blood and . . ." Kathy let the dam break, slowly. Fear, shock, and a couple of other emotions I couldn't quite pinpoint forced their way to the surface. The emotional irrigation made my responsibility level grow. I got up, went to Kathy's side, and sat beside her on the bed. I gently placed her head on my shoulder and comfortingly stroked her hair while she cried.

There was something about a woman in trouble that brought out the best in me. I wanted to help. I wanted to help Kathy. She looked so fragile. I had the distinct feeling she wasn't usually. But right now she was probably more scared than she'd ever been in her life. People watch actors get shot on television all the time. It's antiseptic, neat, and all fits between commercials about mouthwash and deodorant. But in real life it just isn't that way, and if you're ever unfortunate enough to see bullets and blood firsthand, it's one hell of a shock.

"I keep thinking about Edward Smith," said Kathy, slightly recovered now and sipping her juice. I moved back to the chair. "I mean, he was shot. He could be dead now."

"Could be."

"Death's funny, you know," said Kathy, her voice barely cracking.

"How so?" Right off I couldn't think of a lot of funny death jokes, and a funeral is probably the last frontier for comedians.

"My mother died when I was ten years old." I didn't say I was sorry. I hadn't known her mother. I felt bad for anyone growing up without a mother, but I didn't feel at all responsible.

"I always wondered where she was."

"Where?"

"You know, Heaven or Hell. She was here one day, and the next day she was gone. I never got the chance to ask the questions a girl asks her mother. I never got the chance to let her really know how I felt about her."

"How *did* you feel about your mother?"

"I loved her, of course. I . . . no, I'm not sure I loved her at all. She left me and . . ."

Kathy got up from the bed, walked to the window, and looked up into the Hollywood Hills. People looked up there every day, but seldom saw what they were looking for. I didn't know what Kathy was looking for, but if I knew, I'd do what I could to help her find it.

"What do you mean, she left you?" I asked, playing with my beer.

"Oh, I know it doesn't make any sense, but a little girl doesn't always make sense. All I knew was that my mother went away and never came back. I've always wanted to believe she'd come back someday."

I thought I heard a sniff and then she turned back to me stiffly, raised her chin and her lower lip slightly, and gave me an "oh, what-the-hell" smile.

"But it's pretty stupid of me to think my dead mother will just come walking back into my life someday, isn't it, Mr. Carpenter?"

It was a question I didn't get the chance to answer. The shot tore through her and landed in the wall a few inches from my ear. I hit the floor, grabbing at the light switch as I went down. The room went black. I heard moaning. I crawled to the girl. She was hit in the shoulder. It was just a scratch really; no permanent damage done. I said a few comforting things I remembered from a recent *Starsky and Hutch* and bellied my way to the phone next to the bed. It had been a few days since I'd seen anybody shot—it never had made me laugh much.

It did, however, make me feel afraid, and incredibly underpaid. Shootings were a definite strain on me.

I got an operator on the phone who wanted to know if this was an emergency. I assured her that it was. I told her there had been a shooting and that it was your basic life-and-death situation. She responded quickly and put me through to the police. Then the frustration began. A recording came on saying in a calm voice that all the lines were busy and that my call would be answered in the order received. People don't believe that happens, but it does. Finally I got through, gave a man the particulars, hung up, and waited. In the meantime I'd grabbed a heavy piece of wood and slithered my way to the door to stand guard.

A few minutes later I heard footsteps dancing up the stairs. The door burst open and six uniformed officers, three with shotguns, ran into the room and looked at me fiercely.

"I'm one of the *victims*," I said, making no quick movements. "There's a wounded girl over there," I said, pointing to Kathy in the corner.

One of the officers said, "Call for an ambulance and call in a code 4." Another officer, one without a shotgun, holstered his pistol and scampered back downstairs.

I was answering questions and trying to act unafraid when a familiar face appeared at the doorway. "Shoulda figured it was you, Carpenter," said Eddy Price.

"Did I forget our date?"

"I was just a couple streets over when the call came through. What the hell happened here?"

I told Eddy how I'd gotten involved. He just took notes and yawned. If you could get arrested for being boring, this guy would have successive life terms.

Eddy Price and I went way back. We both grew up in Columbus, Ohio, went to Ohio State for about the same three years, and came out to the City of the Angels in

'67. I'd had dreams about being famous—at anything legal. Eddy'd just had dreams. He'd gotten involved with the force through a guy he'd met in a karate class in the late sixties. It gave him some direction. I kind of liked the idea of him being a cop. He was steadily employed and always good for a few bucks when a client's check was late. Or nonexistent.

And now here we were jawboning about attempted murder. I felt a new sense of personal worth—like I'd just been run over by a Rolls instead of a Rambler.

Eddy had had a meteoric rise in the department, much of it due to marrying a captain's daughter. I'd met her once, and though the three of us had only spent that one evening together, it had seemed as though the evening went on as long as Watergate. Eddy and his wife's life together was not exciting. I'd kill myself in the morning if I thought *I'd* have to live it. It was kind of like life in the off-ramp.

I did my stand-up routine for Eddy and the boys for a while. I told them about Kathy St. John's near meeting with the bearded guy who got shot earlier that day at the Old World. They all thought that that was interesting. Finally an ambulance came and took the girl away. Eddy said he thought I wasn't being very helpful. I apologized and told him it was because I didn't know anything. The boys laughed at that one a little. I didn't mean it *that* way.

I found out Kathy was headed for Kaiser Permanente Hospital over on Sunset, near Vermont. I'd been there once before. I'd been sick; had a cold. I'd gone in and taken a number. By the time they'd called my number I was well again. It was one of those kinds of hospitals where the doctors get paid the same amount whether they service anyone or not. It wasn't much motivation. You needed to care. But like most of us, they usually didn't give a shit.

The sun was coming up by the time I was done doing encores for Eddy. The downtown L.A. skyline, what there was of it, was silhouetted against an orange sky. It looked kinda pretty. I wasn't real tired by the time I walked upstairs to my half of a Hollywood Hills duplex, so I fixed myself some tea, put on a Horowitz album, and lay down on the couch.

The phone rang. It was my mother. She never could get the time zone thing straight. It was only about 6:00 A.M. my time, but she was already in a clever mood. She reminded me that I was determined to be a failure. And, unfortunately, that that failing was the only thing I had been successful at in my entire life. She had a point. But I'd heard it all before. My mother was a psychology teacher at Bowling Green State University. She would often claim to have finally gained the ultimate insight into what I must certainly admit had become a life based on the concept that if at first you don't succeed, let it be an omen.

My mom and I had fun for a while talking about how selfish I was, how I never remembered birthdays—the definitive criterion for caring—why I didn't get a *real* job, and how she missed me. It was an old movie by now, but it still made me feel like it was a good thing I had slip-on shoes instead of ties.

Talking with my mother put me in the mood for some breakfast. I ground some coffee, scrambled some eggs, scooped out some cottage cheese, and sat down again on the couch. My phone rang again. It was too late in the morning to be my mother.

"Hello."

"Mr. Carpenter?"

"Yes."

"My name is David St. John."

The name sounded kinda neat—like something you might find printed on a cold capsule.

"I got your name and phone number from the police. My daughter's name is Kathy St. John."

"The girl who was shot last night."

"That's right. She said you are a detective."

"If the price is right." I don't even know why I said that. I'd never said it before. Maybe that's why. It sounded hard, tough. Anyhow, the price would be right if it covered a week's groceries, so it wasn't like I intended to hold him up.

"I'm prepared to pay for your services, Mr. Carpenter."

He was the first in a long time.

"Let's you and me get together and talk about this, Mr. St. John."

"Excellent. Lunch. Today."

"Hold on, let me check my book." I took the opportunity to shovel in another mouthful of eggs. "Looks fine to me. You name the place."

"The Bonaventure Hotel. The Top of Five Restaurant. It's downtown. You know where it is?"

I was a little insulted. I'm a detective. Sure I knew where downtown was. "Yeah."

"The Top of Five then. Twelve noon."

"Good. How will I know you?"

"I'll be wearing a pink carnation."

It sounded a little too romantic for me, but hell, it was a free meal and I never turned down free meals.

"OK, noon. See you then."

The whole business was beginning to take on a new dimension and my interest was starting to build; just like the interest on my loans. It also made me feel good that I'd be seeing Kathy again. Well, at least her father, and it just made sense I'd be seeing her. I could get excited about being her bodyguard. In fact, I was getting excited over a thought similar to that. But I decided to set my alarm and get some sleep before my appointment with St. John.

* * *

The Bonaventure was pretty swank—lots of modern architecture, a lobby big enough to play two Super Bowls in simultaneously, escalators, the works. I got directions to the Top of Five and took my time getting there. I walked in about five minutes late and saw a gray-haired man, nicely dressed, wearing a pink carnation in his lapel, sitting at the bar. He looked like he had been wearing it when he called me and had just happened to look down while he was on the phone and had seen that he had it on. Nothing special for me. He looked like he could afford lunch for both of us without taking out a loan.

"Mr. St. John?"

"Mr. Carpenter," he said, extending his hand.

I then followed him and a guy in a tux, who seemed to know him, or at least respect him, to a table next to a window and a great view. We looked over the menu for a few minutes. The prices looked like my rent receipts. I didn't see fries and a shake, so I ordered scallops doria, and salad instead of soup. I was having a good time.

"Mr. Carpenter, let's get right to the point."

"Suits me fine. I wasn't going anywhere until after lunch."

I learned long ago that rich men didn't have much in the way of a sense of humor—except about things like mergers, stock splits, dividends. And I didn't know any merger jokes.

"I think my daughter is in trouble."

I wasn't sure exactly which problem he was referring to, because, even though I'd only known Kathy St. John for about an hour or so, I could tell she might have quite a few.

"My daughter is a little different, headstrong—though not unlike many young people today," said St. John.

I felt like telling him two things. First of all, I thought

his daughter *was* different, but in a way I didn't think he wanted to hear about it. Secondly, I felt old. What did he mean ' "young people today"? He said it to me as though he were chatting with Father Time. Hell, I'm just twenty-nine years old. Neither thing really seemed all that important, so I bit my tongue.

"Something wrong with your mouth?" asked St. John.

"No, no. Just a nervous habit."

"Sergeant Price says you are an able detective."

"Eddy's a good man." He wasn't a smart man, but he was a good man.

"I'd like to employ you," said St. John, sipping at his water.

The idea sounded great to me.

"What would you like me to do?"

"Well, obviously, my daughter needs protection. I understand from Sergeant Price that a man had asked her to meet him at a restaurant, and that he was shot. And that my daughter asked you to follow her home last night and check out her apartment."

"That's right."

"So why and how did my daughter contact you in particular, Mr. Carpenter?"

I started to notice that St. John never referred to his daughter by her name. I decided I would. "Kathy is a friend of a friend."

"And what is the name of this friend?" asked St. John, reaching for a pen inside his coat pocket.

"You can save your paper. I'm not at liberty to tell you that right now."

"What!" said St. John. It looked as though it had been a while since anyone had said no to him. He certainly wasn't expecting me to break the streak.

"Your daughter is technically a client of mine."

"But, I'm her father," he said, as if those were magic words.

"I'm her detective. Look, there's no need to get upset. I'm sure she'll tell you if you want to know. If she doesn't want you to know, then it would be unethical of me to tell you. I'm sure that you appreciate my position. I'd do the same for you." I was hoping to get the chance.

He took his anger and put it someplace it looked like he was used to putting it; wherever that was, I was sure I'd never want to go there. He put on a social face again and we were back at the masquerade: him as a concerned father, me as a big-time detective.

"I'd like you to protect my daughter. Go with her wherever she goes, within reason, for the next few days. See her safely home at night and stake out the apartment house at night. I'll send a man around to spell you. Just for a few days. Then, when things blow over, if the police haven't found the person responsible for the attack on my daughter—which I doubt they will—then I'd like you to take a crack at it. You can start by picking my daughter up at the hospital after you leave here and taking her to her apartment."

I paused to think over the offer as the waiter brought us our salads.

"I will pay you well. My daughter's safety is very important to me."

I thought it would be unfair to jack up my standard price, take advantage of the situation. But, I did it anyhow. Hell, I was broke and this guy probably polished the chrome on his Bentley steering wheel with hundred dollar bills. I made him an offer we both could live with. "Two hundred dollars a day plus expenses."

He didn't bat an eye. He just took out his wallet. It wasn't bulging; it didn't have to. How many thousand dollar bills did a guy need during the course of a day anyhow? He handed me a card.

"You can reach me at that number anytime day or night. My service knows where I am at all times. And here's five days in advance."

I'm glad he said five days, not one. I didn't have change for a thousand on me. I didn't have change anywhere in the world for a thousand.

When I walked out of the Top of Five I was feeling kinda rich.

I drove from The Bonaventure over to Kaiser Permanente, which was located at the corner of Sunset and Vermont. Kathy's room was on the fourth floor, room 427. It was a private room, naturally. St. John was first class all the way. But I had the suspicion that he would have gotten her a room in the parking lot surrounded by construction workers if that had costed more. I had a crazy dialogue playing in my head: Some woman was saying, "Oh, Mr. St. John, where may I send these flowers to your daughter?" And St. John said, "The most expensive room." And the woman said, "But what's the room number?" And St. John said, "It costs four hundred dollars a day, that's the number." And the woman said, "But I need the room number or else I won't be able to get these flowers to her." And St. John didn't say anything. I had the feeling that St. John hadn't known how to reach his daughter for some time.

It was a nice room, 427. It had more comforts than my Hollywood Hills place, but I had a nicer view at home. The view from the hospital room looked out upon a couple dozen sick people ambling lamely about. My bedroom window looked out upon millions of sick people, but my view had a few trees in between.

The nurse came in. She was a little plump and very nice. Aren't they all? "And what can I do for you, young man?" That tells you she was substantially older than I —at least old enough not to try and disguise her age.

"I'm supposed to meet Kathy St. John. I work for her father. I'm supposed to pick her up and escort her home."

The nurse frowned and her smile puckered into a question there on her lips. "That's odd."

"What is? Isn't she here?"

"Why, no. She left about an hour ago. She said she'd received a call from her father—that she was supposed to meet him downstairs. She followed the proper check-out procedures, and she *is* twenty-one," said the nurse, jamming together all the disclaimers she could think of into one sentence.

"The hospital isn't to blame, Ms. . . .?"

"Fitzpatrick."

"Ms. Fitzpatrick. Tell me, you say she received a call?"

"About an hour and a half ago. She said it was her father and that he had asked her to meet him downstairs where he would have a car waiting. Well, everyone knows Mr. St. John . . . so, well, naturally we tried to oblige."

"Of course. Did anyone meet her downstairs?"

"We don't monitor our patients after they walk out the door. However, I *did* see her get into a black limousine. Mr. St. John drives a limousine—from what I'm told—so we just naturally assumed that everything was all right."

"Did anyone get out of the limousine?"

"Not that I saw. I believe she just opened the door herself and got in. No, wait a minute."

"Yes?"

"Paul Jacobs, an orderly downstairs, helped her to her car and maybe even opened the door for her."

"Is he still on duty?"

"Should be."

"I'd like to speak with him. Could you see if he's still here?"

"Certainly. I'll be right back."

Nurse Fitzpatrick left the room and I looked around

for anything Kathy might have left behind. But I found nothing. About three minutes later Nurse Fitzpatrick padded quietly back into the room.

"He's still downstairs. I told him to meet you in the lobby. His name, Paul Jacobs, will be on his smock."

"Thank you very much."

"The hospital isn't in any kind of trouble about this, is it? I mean, Mr. St. John owns a hefty piece of this place and, well, we want to stay on his good side."

"I'm sure everything's all right," I lied. "Just a mix-up in signals."

Staying on St. John's good side could be a considerable strain, seeing as how I wasn't sure he even had one. Like the dark side of the moon—logic tells you it's there, but nobody sees it.

"Paul Jacobs?"

"That's right, dude," said Jacobs, a tall, thin black man, in his early twenties. His big eyes stared down upon me.

"My name is Ace Carpenter. I work for David St. John." I handed him my card.

"Ace, eh. Strange name. So what can I do for you?"

I'd been kidded about my name nearly every day I used it. Sometimes I used other people's names, just so everyone wouldn't think I was a comedian.

"You helped Kathy St. John to her car today."

"Maybe."

"What do you mean? Oh," I said, reaching for a bill in my pants.

"No. I don't mean that. I help a lot of people to cars. Who's this St. John lady?"

"She may have had her arm in a sling."

"Oh, yeah. That one. Got into a limousine. Not a lot of limousines 'round here."

"Did you see anyone inside the car?"

"Some guy with a beard."

"Front or back seat?"

"He was drivin'."

"Notice anything else?"

"Actually, now that you mention it, he was coughin' a lot. He was hunched over the wheel a little, too. He looked kinda sick to me. Matter a fact, he stopped the car at the end of the driveway and the girl got out, went around to the driver's side, got in, and *she* drove away."

"That's a pretty strange thing for a girl with a wounded wing to do," I said, thinking out loud.

"Unless the bearded guy was in worse shape," said Jacobs.

"Yeah," I said, and thanked him with something better than a handshake. He tucked away the bill, smiled, and said it had been a pleasure. It hadn't been a pleasure for me, but it *had* been informative.

After a call to St. John reaffirming what I already suspected to be true—that he hadn't called Kathy—I called Eddy and told him what was going on. I gave him the nurse's name, as well as Jacobs', and, feeling that I'd done my duty, went on my way. I told Eddy he could find me at Theodore's when he got done. I wanted to get Eddy's take on the vanishing act. So far, it didn't make any sense to me.

Theodore's was on Santa Monica Boulevard, just west of Crescent Heights. The Starwood, a rock and roll club, was on one side. Across the street was a vacant lot that served as the scene of weekend swapmeets. There was a twenty-four-hour bookstore next to the lot. It was the kind of bookstore where, if you wanted to look at pornography, you had to buy a fifty-cent token, which applied toward your purchase—this in order to cut down on degenerate browsers. After the sun went down, the Santa Monica Boulevard streets would be filled with a bizarre sexual electricity. People would be looking for

things they couldn't find at home, in *their* neighborhoods—the kind of things they tried to *keep out* of *their*
neighborhoods—the kind of things they tried to, but
couldn't, keep out of their heads. They would all be out
here at night, young and old. Lots of high-volume
laughter. Not too many smiles.

But this was the middle of the afternoon, and
Theodore's was like the beach at midnight. I ordered a
plate of scrambled eggs and a diet soft drink.

As I was scraping the remainder of my eggs from my
plate with a crust of toast, Eddy Price came in and sat
down opposite me.

"Eatin' lunch, eh?" he said.

"Nope. Playin' tennis," I countered, stuffing the crust
into my mouth.

"You're a funny guy, Ace."

"Thanks, Eddy." Eddy Price was easily amused.
There was a place for him in show business: on an *I Love
Lucy* laugh track.

"St. John's not laughin', though."

"I don't suppose he would be," I said, as I wiped my
mouth with a napkin. "His daughter's disappeared."

"Right."

"So what do you make of it?"

"Not much yet."

"What about the girl gettin' out of the car and drivin'
with her arm in a sling?" I asked.

"The guy was wounded," said Eddy, as positively as
if he were telling me the sun was shining outside.

"What makes you so sure?" I asked, although I'd already figured that part out myself by now.

"Well," he began, but was cut off by the waitress, who
took his order for a chocolate malt and a bagel with
cream cheese. Eddy had picked that up working over on
Fairfax, the Bagel beat.

"The car was found over on Fountain, not a mile
from the hospital. A few kids playin' ball happened to

look inside and there was this guy with a beard just layin' there in the passenger side of the limo."

"Dead?"

"Couldn't get any deader, I guess. It sounds like a sure bet that the guy in the car and the guy who was shot at the Old World are one and the same."

"Anybody see the girl?"

"I got about a dozen guys goin' door to door askin' that very question right now." He smiled. "They're workin' their tails off while you and I sit here goin' over the fine points. Nice, huh?"

Eddy enjoyed being what he was—a cop who could tell a few other cops what to do.

"So who's the stiff?"

"Name's Edward Smith," said Eddy, as his malted and bagels were set in front of him. "He had some big bucks in his wallet when he died. Still there. He seems to be some kind of big deal. He's the founder of Spiritual Psychodynamics. Ever hear of it?"

"Just the name."

"From what we've got on Psychodynamics, it doesn't appear to be no Catholic Church or nothin', but they do all right. Maybe a mil a year, the way I hear it. His primary residence is in Sausalito. He's married, no kids. His group's got a clean bill of health. I mean, they're not into kidnappin' teenagers or sellin' incense at the airport. None of that. It looks pretty legit.

"Oh, by the way, I talked to St. John just before I came over," Eddy continued, sipping his shake.

"And?"

"He wants you to call him immediately."

"I don't suppose he's trying to track me down to give me a raise?"

"Don't be hard on yourself. It wasn't your fault. You showed up for work, it's just that your work didn't show up for you." Eddy smiled.

"Uh ha." He was a fun guy to talk with. "I planned

to go see him after dinner anyhow."

"He told me to tell you he'd be at home. You know where it is?"

"I can find it. How's he taking it?"

"He's upset. A little."

"Does he seem concerned about his daughter's safety?"

"Tell the truth, he seemed more interested in this Smith guy."

"Interesting."

"Not that odd, the way I figure it. I mean, this guy picks his daughter up from the hospital and then dies from a gunshot wound with her in the car. I mean, I'd be interested, too."

"Yeah, I imagine you're right. So where do you go from here?"

"We're still tryin' to get a line on who shot Smith at the Old World. We've come up with a witness who may have seen the sniper drive away."

"Give me a call later tonight if you know something, OK?"

"Sure. You wanna do somethin' tonight? Esther's knockin' down pins—and a few brews—at the Hollywood Lanes, so I'm free. I hate bowling. Jesus, I thought bowling went out in the fifties. And I thought *I* was square."

"You are, Eddy."

He chuckled a little. "I am, I guess. So?"

"So what?"

"You wanna do somethin' tonight?"

"I might be busy. An old girlfriend. But I'll know for sure when you call me tonight. Too late?"

"No. I've got no plans."

I figured that if Eddy had any real dope on Kathy St. John it would be worth the meet.

"Tough thing for a kid to be involved in, a murder,"

said Eddy, as he started making noises with his straw at the bottom of his malted.

"Uh ha."

"Probably just one of her rich friends who got in trouble, called her for help and died on her. Tough. Real tough. Probably runnin' scared right now."

I asked for my check, left a bill on the table, and told Eddy I looked forward to his call.

Right then, though, I had a date. With an old girlfriend.

When she opened the door I found myself confronted by two rather large, slightly sagging breasts. I'm not a tit man. Legs are what I really like. But Penny liked to walk around half-naked and, well, her breasts were naturally where my attention was first attracted. Lots of movement.

"Hi, Ace," said Penny. She wore panties now. She had become conservative since her thirtieth birthday. "Don't just stand there. Come on in."

I did. She had a nice place—nothing fancy, but it had charm. It was a carriage house apartment over a garage behind a ritzy house in West Hollywood. It had hand-carved woodwork, built-in bookcases, and lots of trees trying to sneak in the open windows. The floors were hardwood. She still had a mattress on the living room floor, which served as a couch. A little incense burner decorated the coffee table. A recently used hash pipe lay nearby. A metaphysical library lined one wall of her living room. If it had to do with the spirit or the mind, Penny had experienced it, read about it, or been it. And each trip was better than the last, or so she always told me. Her life was constantly in flux—a flower forever unfolding toward the light of consciousness. For my money, she had long ago begun to fold around herself and wouldn't know the truth if it slept with her.

I had slept with her. It was neither the truth nor a lie. But Penny always made a place in her life for those uncommitted, gray-area types like myself. Our paths had crossed one night when I was playing guitar at Theodore's. She had come in with some straight-looking guy, and during the course of the evening both she and her date had been attentive and appreciative. I always noticed attentive patrons. To most of the Theodore regulars, I was just live Muzak. I liked anyone who bought me drinks regardless of whether or not they were music lovers. The combination of the two was almost overwhelming.

About midnight they'd left and I'd settled in to singing John Denver's "Take Me Home, Country Roads" about every other song—the last set was usually just requests. When I'd been about to finish, the waitress, who particularly liked John Denver songs, had come smiling in my direction. On her cocktail tray was a note. It was from Penny, and it had a phone number on it. After my set, I'd called the number and she'd asked me what my plans were after I'd gotten done playing. I'd said I didn't have any and she'd asked me to come over to her place.

I'd knocked on her door about 1:30 in the morning. She'd opened it wearing a see-through negligee. For a minute or two I'd thought I was in the middle of a *Playboy* cartoon. But I'd grabbed a couple touchstones of reality and assured myself that even if it weren't reality, I was bound to have a good time. The sex had been something this side of excellent, but we'd become good friends afterward.

"Thanks for the referral," I said now, as I took a seat on the mattress/couch.

"Referral?" she said, sitting down on the floor opposite me.

"Kathy St. John."

"Oh, Kathy. I just told her you'd located Edgar and Cindy."

"Finding two cats is hardly the measure of a good detective, but she seemed to buy it."

"Kathy and I've become good friends over the past couple months. Tea? I've got some made."

She always had some made. I hated tea. "No, thanks. How about a beer?"

"You know I don't drink beer."

"Just wondered if you'd picked up any other bad habits besides wearing panties."

She sipped on her tea without answering and smiled a little.

"How did you meet Kathy?" I asked.

"She was dating a friend of mine. I met Kathy at a party and we hit it off. We visit each other for tea, conversation, that sort of thing, a few times a week. Why? What's going on?"

"You referred her to me. Didn't she tell *you?*"

"Nope. There are certain things she wouldn't talk about. And one thing a friend doesn't do is force another friend to talk about things she doesn't want to talk about."

"Admirable," I said, and yawned.

"You tired?"

"No. Did Kathy ever mention a guy named Edward Smith to you?"

"No."

"Did you ever see her with a guy who wore a beard?"

"Nope. Hey," she said, as if she'd just remembered something, "Edward Smith, the founder of Spiritual Psychodynamics, has a beard.

"As a matter of fact, Kathy called me yesterday and asked me if I had any books on SP. That's what made me think of it."

"What is SP all about anyhow?" I knew I'd asked the right person.

"Well, Smith has two SP centers, one in L.A. and one in San Francisco. His main headquarters are in San

Francisco. But he comes down here about twice a month to give lectures and check up on the operation. He used to be a psychologist—in London, I think. Made his reputation over there and set up shop in 'Frisco about four years ago. He's not big time, you know, like the Maharishi or somebody like that, but he's very together. He's tried to stay out of the limelight as much as possible. Usually the leader of each center takes responsibility for what goes on there."

"You ever go?" I asked, already knowing the answer. I just wanted to get a chance to say my line.

"Sure. I've been to the center a bunch of times. It's not an exclusive-type religion like a lot of 'em where it's 'us against them.' You can go to other religious groups' meetings and still come back to SP."

"Just as if you were a free person," I said.

"Yes," she said, as if she were serious. I think she was.

"Do you know Edward Smith personally?"

"No. Never met him," she said.

I'd figured as much. But I'd just wanted to make it official that Kathy had lied to me when she told me she had agreed to meet Smith at the Old World Restaurant because he was a friend of Penny's.

"So what goes on at an SP center?"

"It's mainly group-oriented stuff: sensitivity sessions, awareness groups geared toward expanding consciousness."

I had a picture of that. A room full of people sitting around in a circle slapping and verbalizing each other into a spiritual frenzy for a hundred dollars a day. It sounded like a lot of fun—unless you were sane.

"Can I borrow one of your books on SP?"

"Sure. And I know just the one," she said, getting up and going to her metaphysical archives. She found what she was looking for and brought me a volume entitled *You Are Love*. I felt more like Love's distant cousin,

Lust, but I was willing to contemplate a reunion.

"Penny, could you give me the phone number and address of the guy Kathy was dating?"

"Sure." She sat down next to a table, reached in its drawer, and pulled out a little black address book. She leafed through it, found what she was looking for, and wrote something on a piece of paper.

"Here," she said, handing me the paper.

"Thanks."

"Is Kathy all right?" asked Penny, a little concerned.

"Sure. I think so. I just haven't seen her in a few hours. We had an appointment and she didn't show up. That's all." That was far from all, but it wasn't necessary to worry Penny with details like murder.

I looked at the picture of Smith on the back of the book she had lent me.

I was looking at a dead man.

I took a right on Sunset, about the place I usually turn my head to look up the hill and admire the view and the palaces of the tanned and rich. I followed Sunset Hills Drive up to Blue Jay Way. I remembered that the Beatles had written a song by that name when they'd leased a house on that street. I was great on rock'n'roll trivia. In my preteens I'd collected baseball cards and memorized batting averages, E.R.A.s, won–lost records, and so on. When I got older and interested in music, I began to pick up information about rock'n'roll stars. I could name all the members of the Dave Clark Five, Herman's Hermits, Gerry and the Pacemakers, et al.; I was awesome on the topic of British rock'n'roll.

When I got to the top of the hill I could see downtown L.A. on my left and the ocean on my far right. It was evening now. And though I could see the moon rolling through the clouds like a bowling ball in search of celestial pins, there wasn't a star to be seen. I knew they were there. I remembered they always came out at night. I remembered that from my days in Ohio. But living in Hollywood, the only stars I'd seen I'd paid to see.

St. John's place was set back off the street about a hundred feet. A black driveway connected it with the rest of the world. The house and the man both seemed not to care if that connection were broken.

An Oriental opened the door on my second ring and ushered me into the foyer, where he would have taken my hat and coat if I'd had a hat or a coat. Instead he informed me that Mr. St. John would be out shortly and that I should have a seat in the living room.

He showed me into a room painted rich with a fireplace, a couple of expensive-looking paintings, a comfortable-looking leather eight-piece sectional, and thick white shag carpeting. On the walls were pictures of St. John with numerous political figures, movie stars, and other entertainment notables. I'd never heard of David St. John before that day, but if you could go by the pictures, his would be a two-ton name to drop at any influential gathering.

After a time sufficient for me to digest the carefully constructed atmosphere, St. John made his entrance. I decided not to get up. I also decided not to bow. I think he would have been equally at ease with either gesture.

"Mr. Carpenter," he said, extending his hand. Even though I knew I was being manipulated, I was pleased, even proud, that he remembered my name. *My* name stashed in the same memory bank with Sylvester Stallone, Muhammad Ali, Bruce Lee, and Richard Nixon. Kind of an uneven Hall of Fame, but I was glad to be inducted. We shook hands.

"May I be blunt, Mr. Carpenter?" He wasn't really asking my permission, but simply preparing the context for something that was unpleasant for him to say.

"Certainly. And you may call me Ace."

He smiled an uncomfortable smile, like that was pretty low on his list of things he'd like to do, and sat down.

"I know a little about you, Mr. . . . Ace"—it wasn't an easy thing for him to do, to be this familiar . . . with me—"and your record as a detective. And while it has no blemishes on it to speak of"—interesting choice of words, I thought; what about not to speak of?—"your experience *is*, shall we just say, limited for such a serious matter as this."

We shan't. He did.

"Nonetheless, I've decided to retain your services."

"What changed your mind?"

"In fact, it was Sergeant Price. He said he knew you, knew your work, and said that you were a fine detective. Also, he felt that since you were already involved in the case, and if I were going to hire a private detective anyway, I might as well keep you on."

"That was nice of Eddy." I meant it. But after I thought about it a little, I realized Eddy had been hinting around about some money I owed him. And since I wasn't working . . . well, we all look out for ourselves one way or another.

"Besides, Sergeant Price assured me he'd watch over you in case you got into something you couldn't handle."

It was getting less nice of Eddy all the time. But it was money and that was just the thing that would make a few people I still almost knew pretty happy. For some people, money was like a magic brush that animated the world around them, made it dance. For me, money was like a bandage healing an ugly wound.

I recovered my pride somewhat and said, "You could make my job easier by answering a few questions."

"Certainly. Anything. I want my daughter back, Mr. Carpenter."

We were both aware he had shied away from saying

"Ace," but that was all right. Maybe it was better that way. I wasn't sure I'd want St. John as a friend any more than he'd want to introduce me to the President.

I took out a notebook and flipped over the first few pages, which were filled with lists of things to do: take out the garbage, pay phone bill, wake up at seven, replace lightbulb in closet. Why I saved the pages I didn't know. I made a note to myself on tomorrow's list: tear out pages of lists in front of notebook.

"Let's start at the beginning. When was the last time you saw or spoke with your daughter?"

About this time St. John's manservant brought in a tray of drinks and appetizers and set them on the table between St. John and me. St. John nodded to the Oriental, the Oriental accepted the acknowledgment, and exited, presumably to prepare the next pampered step in St. John's daily routine. Though I was flippant about such a lifestyle, I'd trade it for mine in a second if anyone offered.

"In fact, you saw her after I did," he said, after his manservant had left. "When she sought you out at the, ah . . ."

"Mirabelle's."

"Yes. We'd had dinner the night before. Tuesday night. It was a late supper, about 10:30 P.M."

"Where was that?"

"The California Club, I believe. Yes, the California Club. The prime rib was superb, the Beaujolais too pedestrian for my taste."

I wrote down the name of the restaurant, but left out the review.

"Did your daughter appear disturbed about anything?"

"No, not disturbed." He was searching for the right word. "She was inquisitive. She was interested in *me*. For a change," he added, sipping at his cocktail.

"How so?"

"Well, my daughter is self-centered. That may not be a nice thing to say, but it's true. She's never cared two cents about *my* work, what *I* do. As long as her needs—whims, really—were fulfilled, then that was all she wanted to know."

"What did you talk about Tuesday night?"

"She asked about my life, my work, how I got started, how I met her mother; lots of things I'd have been only too glad to share with her a thousand times before. If she'd asked."

"And where is your wife now?"

"Ah, a good woman, Ellen. I'm afraid she left us long ago."

"Kathy told me her mother passed away when Kathy was ten."

"Yes, I'm sorry to say. A skiing accident in Zurich."

The rich even died with class, I thought. People I knew died of tumors or coronaries in Pomona or Madison, Wisconsin. A skiing accident in Zurich. Jesus! Probably St. John would die taking a bullet for the President of the United States. Well, at least my obit would say I'd worked for him.

St. John picked up an hors d'oeuvre from the tray and put it in his mouth while I wrote a few notes.

"When did your daughter move away from home?"

"That's hard to say. It's a matter of degrees; she moved out a little at a time. I've spared no expense where my daughter is concerned. She's been enrolled in the best schools in the world since she was ten years old."

"She moved out when she was ten?" I asked, trying not to sound incredulous.

"Certainly not. She came home during breaks, vacations; occasionally I'd join her for a holiday somewhere. She often spent part of her summers here. We were as close as father and daughter *should* be," he said, as he took another sip from his cocktail.

I was wondering where St. John had gotten his information on just how close such a relationship should be. I looked around the room again at the pictures. One could easily assume that St. John was a bachelor, a man without a family. There were no pictures of his daughter, and the women he was with in the pictures were certainly too young to be anyone's wife.

"When did your wife die?"

"In 1968. December of that year. Ellen—that was her name—and my daughter and I often took a winter holiday together at a chalet in Zurich owned by an acquaintance of mine."

"What was your friend's name?"

St. John looked at me as if I'd just asked him to recite the alphabet backward. "I beg your pardon?"

"I just ask any question that comes into my mind. I sort out the meat later. Humor me, all right?"

"All right. A little." He lifted his eyebrows and probably silently cursed Eddy Price and his recommendations.

"My friend's name was Simon Bernstein, Jr. He was the son of the man in whose practice I got my start in corporate law. Simon Jr. and I were buddies in school, UCLA, and before that, at Glendale High School." He didn't smile at the recollection.

"Where is Mr. Bernstein now?"

"You are becoming tedious, Mr. Carpenter. I cannot see the slightest bearing of such information upon the disappearance of my daughter. But I'll answer your question, which I hope will be the last on the topic. I don't know where Simon is. He took up practice somewhere in the East some years back. I occasionally get a Christmas card from him, but we are not in touch. There. Are you happy?"

I wasn't ready to do cartwheels out the front door, but

I was feeling OK. "Would you mind if I took a look at your daughter's old room?"

"My daughter has not maintained a room in this house for many years."

"I see. Then do you think you could call the owner of her apartment building and have him let me in to take a look around?"

"No problem. I'm the owner. I'll call the manager and tell him to expect you."

"Fine. I'll go over there in a couple hours. I've got a stop to make first."

I got up. The Oriental appeared out of thin air and led me to the door. The door closed heavily behind me, as if the world to which it opened was a place I didn't belong in. Maybe I didn't. Maybe I didn't want to.

It was about 7:00 P.M. when I wedged myself into my VW and headed down the hill into Hollywood. I wanted to see SP headquarters with my own eyes.

There it was. Right there on the Sunset Strip next to an obscene flashing sign that depicted a disco singer in various stages of undress. I kinda liked the sign. SP's yellow and blue colors were on their sign outside and the people inside wore yellow t-shirts and blue pants. They looked like an intramural high school baseball team.

Inside, the scene was subdued chaos. One girl sat interviewing a prospective SPer. Several young men and women were on their phones in animated conversations. Lots of talk about how easy money was to get if you *really* wanted it. I was only hearing one side of those conversations, but they all sounded pretty much the same. Desperate. Maybe they needed new outfits. Other staff members were typing, filing, or just sitting around. One of the latter spotted me. A smile slipped into gear on her face and she came to reel me in. I had nothing to do, I had money in my pocket, so I took the hook.

"Good evening," she said, with a smile so bright I wished I'd worn my sunglasses.

"Seems fine so far."

"Could be better, though, right?" she queried, as if she knew something about me that she was about to reveal.

Actually, it could have been better, but a Royal Cappuccino at Sarno's would have taken care of that nicely.

"My name is Judy Wise."

"Hi," I said.

"Why don't you come over here to my desk and have a seat."

I couldn't think of a good reason not to, so I tailed along.

"I'd like to ask you a few questions," she said, picking up a pen and writing a couple things on a piece of paper.

"All right."

The preliminary questions had to do with my name and address.

I made up the address. I didn't want junk mail filling my mailbox for the rest of my life. After that, the questioning began in earnest.

"Are you happy with your life?"

"My mother isn't," I said.

She smiled as though I'd given her the right answer.

"Do you believe you have some control over your own destiny?"

"To a certain extent. But nothing a .38 couldn't put a stop to in a hurry," I replied in my best Bogie.

"A .38?"

"A bullet," I explained.

"I see." I could see that no one had given her that answer in a while. She took an extra long look at me, though her smile remained in place. She crossed her legs so that her thighs were now visible to me. Although it was not an invitation, her body language told me that she was willing to get acquainted.

"Do you have trouble controlling your thoughts?"

It was as if she had read my mind. "Sometimes." Now that was an answer she looked like she'd heard before.

"Do you believe in God?"

"As long as He believes in me, I'm satisfied." My freshman philosophy class had finally paid off. I'd waited years to answer a question about the existence of God.

"Do you believe that honesty is important?"

"With certain exceptions. Like when dealing with the government or when making love." I'd have to say that she thought that was kinda cute.

"Do you have any feelings about Edward Smith, the founder of SP?"

"I'd have to meet him before I'd ask him to move in, but I really don't know enough about him to feel one way or the other." I realized that by her casual expression when she said Smith's name, word of his death had not yet filtered down to the peons. And I didn't want to be the one to break the news.

"What was your reason for coming here today?"

"I wanted to use the phone."

She looked at me strangely.

"I'm just kidding," I said. "I was just walking by, and I'd heard about SP and decided to do a little personal investigation."

"Investigation?" The word seemed to slap her face.

"Just a personal investigation. You know, like finding out for myself what SP is all about. It might help make my life a little better." I choked on the words, but they bandaged her wound.

"I see." The smile came back and sat there on her pretty face. "I'd like you to see a film we have about SP. It explains all about the therapy, how it works, and what it can do for you."

"Sounds OK to me," I said.

"All right, if you'll just have a seat over there," she said, pointing to a seat next to a bust of Edward Smith, "I'll call you when the next showing is ready. It won't be long—about ten minutes."

I left the Cheshire smile and sat down on the couch. The reading material was predictable. All the books and pamphlets were by Edward Smith. He took a good picture. And it was the same handsome likeness on all the books on the table. Most of the books had catchy esoteric titles, but the one that caught my eye was *Recovering Past Abilities Through Reincarnation Therapy*. I used to have this idea that I was a thief in a past life, and that if I could go back to that particular past life, I might be able to remember where I stashed some money. After a swift perusal of the volume, I picked up a price list and found that in order for me to be able to sign up for SP therapy, I'd first have to find the treasure.

The next hour or so was pretty boring. I saw the film, which told me a bit about the life of Edward Smith. He was a college graduate, a world traveler. In the late sixties Smith started SP in Europe. In one film segment, Smith, smiling, said that he would like to give away his spiritual technology free of charge, but that people just won't take something for nothing. Obviously he had never asked me if I wanted any. I feel genuinely at ease while receiving a gift. In fact, I often feel guilty about *spending* so much for the things I *do* buy. To tell the truth, I'd heard most of the spiel before, even the "unique mind technology," from at least a half dozen similar groups in the past decade.

I left SP headquarters about 9 P.M. and drove over to Kathy's apartment. As I passed through the living, dying, breathing, wheezing, neon pornographic magazine that was Hollywood, I saw the hookers in their shorts and high heels ... the pimps in their blatant, cocky dress and transportation ... the corner newspaper vendors getting their inflated prices for handing out the nightly ration of bad news.

I drove by an old hotel over on Cahuenga where a derelict I'd noticed three days in a row was still standing facing the north wall of the hotel. A vacant lot wallowed next to the hotel. The derelict seemed to be arguing with the wall. Occasionally he would impotently strike it with his fist. Empty bottles were strewn around the pathetic pugilist, whose hands were bleeding. Tonight as I drove past I saw a group of kids standing around rooting the old man on as he pounded the flailing shadow on the red-smudged cement. Finally, the old man threw a wild, all-out punch at the wall. The impact and the pain knocked him on his ass. The boys cheered and a couple of them threw the old man a few coins. The derelict smiled a drunken, toothless grin and crawled for the change in the dirt among the cluttered garbage. At that moment he seemed a less unfamiliar figure. In fact, in many ways he was like a lot of people in Hollywood, except maybe he had lower expectations and therefore suffered less disappointment.

I remembered Kathy St. John's apartment from the night before. Tonight it seemed like a deserted tomb that even the ghosts didn't want.

I moved through the hallway into Kathy's bedroom, switched on the light, and looked around. It was all pretty much the same as it had been the night before, except Eddy and the boys had messed it up a little. I decided to look through the drawers. I did have St. John's permission, but then, they weren't St. John's drawers. St. John had a way of talking that made whatever he said sound beyond the law and understanding of mortals. Kathy was mortal. Almost a little too mortal last night.

But I liked her better than her old man, anyhow. Maybe I was mortal, too. But it was too late in the evening and too close to my last drink to start thinking about that one.

The dresser drawers were full of women's things: panties, stockings, bras, t-shirts, shorts. The drawers of a desk next to a window contained an address book, smoking papers, a picture album, a daily calendar. I decided it might be better to take a few notes than to commit a crime by taking the contents. First I looked at the daily calendar under Wednesday, October 10th, the day she was supposed to meet with Smith at the Old World. In a scrawl it read: *Meet Linda at noon for lunch.*

Next I quickly perused the address book. There were four Lindas. I wrote down each one's name and phone number.

The past few weeks, according to her calendar, seemed pretty dull. It figured that a woman as good-looking as Kathy had to have a few male friends. The photo album turned up a bunch of recent pictures under which read captions such as "Bill and me at Alice's, August, '79," "Bill and me on Josh's yacht, June '79," and so on. The name that Penny had given me was Bill Jamison. It was a good bet he was the same Bill as the one in the photos. Still, I scanned the address book for Bills and Williams and found a few. I was also aware that Kathy might not feel that it was necessary to write her steady date's name and number in her book. I wrote down the names and numbers of two Bills and one William.

I put the scrapbook, the address book, and the calendar back in the drawer. Just as I was turning to leave the room I had a crazy idea. It was the oldest damned trick in the book; every kid over nine who watches TV knows it, but what the hell. I sat down on the edge of Kathy's bed and turned on the light on the night table. A phone, a pad, and a pencil were also on the stand. I took the pencil and lightly rubbed its sharp point over the top sheet of paper.

"I'll be damned," I said out loud. I could make out a phone number. It was a San Francisco or Bay Area number. I could tell because it was in the 415 area code. I copied it down, put it in my pocket, and turned off the lights.

I left Kathy's apartment, walked out into the city streets, toward my bar, and I felt like one hell of a detective.

I awoke of my own volition the next morning—as opposed to my mother's. The sun was shining, as usual. I got out of bed and walked through the morning paces: relieve bladder, brush teeth, heat water, open drapes, get paper, brew coffee. After some scrambled eggs I decided on a course of action for lunch.

"Hello, may I speak to Judy Wise?"

"This is she," said the voice on the other end of the phone.

"This is Ace Carpenter. I talked with you yesterday."

She laughed a little. She remembered.

"I'm going to be in the neighborhood around lunchtime. How about you and me grabbing a bite together?"

"Well, I don't know, Mr. Carpenter."

"Ace."

"Ace. I don't usually go out with people who are not on the SP ladder to freedom."

I thought about lying to her and telling her that she had it in her power to put one of my gumshoes on the lower rung, but I told her the truth instead—at least part of it.

"Look, I'm sure you've heard about Edward Smith by now." I figured it was safe. It was in the morning paper.

She paused a few seconds, then said, "Yes, it's been

on the radio and in the papers. We believe Edward was murdered by the government."

"I'm a detective. Maybe I could help."

She thought it over for a minute, then finally said, "All right. Let's have lunch. Meet me at the Source at one."

"One P.M.," I confirmed, and hung up.

The Source was the ultimate in vegetarian chic restaurants. You could eat outside among the noxious gases emitted by passing cars and bask in the shadows of lurid record album billboards and be seen washing down some mung beans with a glass of expensive carrot juice. It wasn't my idea of an ideal lunch, but I didn't argue. I arrived about five minutes before Judy did and procured us a table. I waved her over when she arrived.

"You are a very spiritual person, do you know that?" said Space Cadet Wise sincerely after we'd both ordered.

"Yeah, well, that may be, but it's not important right now."

"But it is. Spirituality is *always* important. There is no time but now," she said.

Things were not going in the direction I'd intended, so I decided to give them a push. "Let's talk about Edward Smith."

She shifted gears smoothly. "They're trying to discredit SP."

"They?"

"The forces of darkness."

"The forces of darkness have never taken the rap for anything, so unless you can give me names, we might as well skip the carrot juice."

"The government is against freedom of speech and religious worship."

"So what else is new?" I said. "The government is against freedom period, but it's not a crime to oppress a nation."

"The FBI, the CIA, the FDA, and the DAR are all trying to destroy SP."

"The DAR? The Daughters of the American Revolution?"

"Is that what it stands for?"

"Yes."

"Are you sure?"

"Yes."

"Well, maybe not them, but the others are definitely trying to subvert SP's followers."

I didn't say it, but I thought, why waste the time? Just turn them loose on each other.

"This is all quite amusing," I said, "and don't think I don't have a sense of humor, but you said that you would give me some help in finding out who murdered your boss."

"I am. The government murdered him. Take my word for it. They wanted him bad because he had the technology of truth, and with that truth he could expose their falseness and corruption."

I was getting pretty frustrated and decided to try another tack. "Who in SP was the closest to Edward Smith?"

"His secretary, Kitty Jacobs, and his attorney, Simon Bernstein."

That last name rang a bell.

"Is Mr. Bernstein a local lawyer?"

"Oh, yes. His offices are in Century City."

I called Bernstein's office, dropped St. John's name as well as Smith's, and got a 4:00 P.M. appointment. It was only 2 then, so I had some time to kill. I decided to grab a cup of coffee and a bite at a little cafe in Venice that fronted the beach and the ocean. Roller-skating young women in shorts, displaying long tanned legs, danced erotically past as I dipped my English muffin into a spreading river of poached yolk. The coffee was all right. I'd just read the night before that coffee depletes certain chemicals in the brain that promote intelligence and memory. I'd read the same thing about alcohol, too, but I couldn't remember where.

As I was paying my bill I noticed there was a commotion coming from a nearby pier. I asked a few questions; it seemed that some guy had committed suicide by roller-skating off the end of the pier into the Pacific Ocean. I guess roller skates and a pier were Venice's answer to Valium and the Golden Gate Bridge.

Bernstein's Century City office was pretty plush. The elevator opened up in front of his receptionist, who asked the usual questions, to which I replied appropriately. She asked me to be seated. The Muzak was fine, the magazines too financially oriented for me—give me a magazine with lots of pictures. I could see a conference room through an open door. The room was larger than my whole apartment. The suite was so quiet I had the feeling that if a bomb exploded in there, it would whisper.

Finally a buzzer buzzed and I was instructed by the receptionist as to how to find my way to Bernstein's office. It wasn't hard, but I thought about tearing up pieces of paper and leaving a trail behind so I'd be able to find my way out.

After shaking hands, Bernstein sat down behind his desk and eyed me warily. He motioned for me to seat myself in front of the desk. One whole wall of his office was glass. He had a view from Century City looking west to the ocean. Maybe with a telescope he could have seen the tragedy at the pier. But then, Bernstein didn't look like the kind of guy who'd be interested in roller-skate suicides.

"You told my secretary that you represent David St. John."

The name seemed to mean something to him. It

should. According to St. John, they used to be close friends.

"I wasn't lying," I said. "You can check it out if you wish."

"I did."

"Didn't you trust me?"

"It is not a question of trust, Mr. Carpenter. It is a matter of certainty. After all, Mr. Smith is—was—a very good friend and client of mine."

"Mr. St. John said you and he used to be friends."

"That is correct," he said flatly.

"He told me that you were practicing in the East."

"Not that it is any business of yours, but I did live in New York for a few years during the early seventies. But I came back here in '77."

"I take it that you and Mr. St. John are no longer friends."

"Things change, Mr. Carpenter. Life changes people. David and I changed and went in different directions. Simple as that. And that is all I intend to say on the subject."

"I'd like to ask you a few questions about Edward Smith, if I may."

"You may *ask* anything you like. I will answer only those questions I feel are appropriate to answer," said Bernstein. He lit his pipe and curled some smoke toward the ceiling.

"When did you find out that Edward Smith had been killed?"

"I have eyes and ears. It's almost a media event," he said sardonically.

"When was the last time you saw Edward Smith?"

"Tuesday night. He was lecturing at his center over on Sunset. He has a small two-story building near the corner of Sunset and Doheny. The second story serves as a small lecture hall."

He paused, took the pipe from his mouth, and looked

me in the eye. "How does Edward's death concern David St. John?"

"You know from the news accounts that Edward Smith was the man who was shot in front of the Old World Restaurant on Wednesday," I said.

"Yes."

"Smith allegedly phoned Kathy St. John, David St. John's daughter, and arranged for her to meet him for lunch at the Old World Wednesday afternoon. He was arriving at the restaurant to meet her when he was shot. Now Kathy's disappeared and Smith is dead."

I left out the part about Smith picking her up at the hospital. I didn't have to give Bernstein a report. I just had to give him enough information to get him to understand that he ought to cooperate.

"I see," he said, puffing a little harder.

"Did anything unusual happen at the lecture Tuesday night?"

"Absolutely not."

"Did Edward seem disturbed to you?"

"Actually, now that you mention it, Edward did seem strangely distant later that night. The lecture itself went smoothly. He was his usual charismatic self. After the lecture Edward went into the audience, as he always does, and answered questions on a one-to-one basis. Each lecture attracts an audience of about fifteen to twenty-five people. Tuesday evening after the rest of the audience had gone, Edward sat in the corner with one young woman. I remember that at the time I thought something seemed to be wrong. Usually, while talking to members of the audience, Edward was even more charismatic than when he lectured. He always smiled, put up a good front. Good PR man, Edward was. Well, anyhow, he seemed deeply engaged in a serious, even angry conversation with this woman. If anything, it looked as if she was lecturing *him,* not the other way around. He seemed upset. In fact, we were all supposed to go out to dinner together afterward—that was why I was there that night—but Edward cancelled without any good reason and just left. It was not like him at all."

"What did the girl look like?"

"She looked as if she had been around. She had a nice figure, dark hair; in her early twenties, I would say. She wore clothes that made her look young."

"What kind of clothes?"

"Those pants, kind of shiny, skintight. Not like jeans-skintight; more like leotard-skintight. They were blue and she wore a red tube top. She was actually quite attractive in a tawdry sort of way. She also wore spiked high-heeled shoes. She was a strange one, all right. But that kind wanders in all the time there on Sunset. The SP headquarters are very near the Rainbow Bar and Grill, the Roxy, and the Whiskey. At least her hair wasn't pink and green."

"You said, 'we were all going to dinner.' Who's we?"

"Edward, myself, and Edward's secretary, Kitty Jacobs."

"Smith was married," I said. It was not a question. It was bait. I just threw it out to see what I'd catch.

"Yes, he was. However, he chose to keep his private life private while he was alive. I would imagine he would want to do so even more now. His wife lives in the Bay Area, which was Edward's full-time place of residence. That's all I'm going to tell you about Edward's wife."

"How can I get in touch with Kitty Jacobs?"

"She traveled with Edward. Therefore, she should still be in town. She and Edward were not scheduled to go back up north until tomorrow. In fact, Edward was supposed to come in today to sign some papers. Kitty and Edward usually stayed at the Beverly Hills Hotel. In separate rooms—I can assure you on that point," said Bernstein emphatically.

I wasn't sure why Bernstein was so emphatic about it. Maybe he was just going out of his way not to soil the memory of the dead. In any case, I'd gotten all I was going to get, or needed, for the moment from Bernstein. I shook his hand again, took a last look down upon the world through his window, and descended a couple dozen stories into the smoggy and overpopulated streets of Los Angeles.

The Beverly Hills Hotel was about a mile and a half west of the business district of the Sunset Strip, just beyond the mansion where the Arab put pubic hair on the statues. The hotel itself was painted flesh pink but had no pubic hair—on the outside. It did, however, have the Polo Lounge. And many of the Polo Lounge's patrons were avid pubic hair enthusiasts.

I walked past the chic shops that lined the corridors leading to the main lobby. I'd been there before, so it was no big deal going to the hotel that had had a novel written about it. The carpet was thick and soft and I walked silently through the same lobby that Gable, Lombard, and the rest had walked through. *I* didn't have to worry about being recognized. I had to worry about proving who I was.

"Is a Ms. Kitty Jacobs registered here?" I asked the man standing behind the desk. He looked at me and his eyes said, "You can't be a guest here!"

"I work for Edward Smith and . . ." I lied.

"Oh, of course." The man's mood changed. He put on his sympathetic mood. He appeared to have a closet full of moods, all of which fit, none of which were real. The man was paid to look as if he cared. "We are very sorry to hear what happened to Mr. Smith."

"It was a blow to us all," I said. "Now, if you'll give me Ms. Jacobs' room number, we have some important matters to discuss."

"Of course, Mr. . . .?"

"Hall." I looked around and that's what I saw. A hall.

"Mr. Hall, Ms. Jacobs is in room 115. Shall I call ahead?"

"No. That won't be necessary. Thank you." I turned and left the desk and glided silently down a few more corridors until I arrived at a door with a couple of ones and a five on it.

"Ms. Jacobs?" I asked of the woman who opened the door.

"Yes."

"My name is Carpenter. I'm a private detective. I just came from Simon Bernstein's office and he told me I could find you here. I'd like to ask you a couple of questions about Mr. Smith." I showed her my identification. She nodded.

The expression on her face confirmed that she knew her boss was dead. Resignedly, she let me come in. The room was bright and cheery, with a view that opened onto the tennis courts and cabanas. She sat down in a powder blue crushed velvet chair and I took a similar one opposite her. There was a bottle of Pernod, half empty rather than half full, sitting on the night table next to the bed. Her eyes, dark and bloodshot, had registered the tragedy. She looked about forty. She was tall, had a nice figure, dark hair, a rather prominent nose. A pair of glasses dangled on a chain around her neck. She was conservatively dressed in a dark knee-length skirt and a white blouse. The jacket that went with the skirt hung on a hanger inside the open closet.

"Are you involved in looking for the person who killed Edward?" she asked finally.

"Indirectly." I told her what I'd told Bernstein.

"I've never heard Edward mention Kathy St. John, or David St. John, for that matter," she said, lighting a cigarette. It was black with a gold filter. She offered me one, but I refused.

"And you know him quite well," I said.

"Quite well," she said, smiling a little. "But not the way you might think. Our relationship was purely business in nature. Mr. Smith's married, you know."

"I know," I replied. I also knew of no reason a married man couldn't fool around with another woman. Sure it might be immoral—or it might not be—but it happened all the time. I decided not to go into the moral questions of our time; especially the moral values of Californians. Midwesterners, maybe; I'd have time for that. But I might never have enough time to discuss the moral values currently in vogue on the West Coast.

"When was the last time you saw Edward Smith?"

"Tuesday night. He was giving a lecture at the Sunset office."

"Did he seem upset about anything?"

"No."

"What about after the lecture? Did anything happen to upset him?"

She hesitated. "No."

"I understand that Edward was supposed to join you and Mr. Bernstein for dinner."

"That's right."

"Did you go to dinner with Mr. Smith after the meeting?"

"No," she said.

"Why not?"

She stubbed out her cigarette and looked out toward the tennis courts, as if searching for the ghost of her boss, who would have the right answer. Finally she said, "Edward was very tired, that's all."

"And he didn't appear upset to you?"

"No."

"Wasn't he talking for a long time with a woman after the lecture?"

Kitty Jacobs wasn't used to lying. She did a bad job of it. "Maybe. I don't know. I don't keep tabs on what

Edward does—did—all the time."

But she *had* noticed the girl, *and* that the girl had upset her boss. That much was certain. That she wasn't going to talk about it with me just now was also certain. But that was all right. Sometimes people's lies were more revealing than their truths. Usually people had a reason to lie. Kitty Jacobs had a reason, and I planned to find out what it was.

"Are you going to be in town long?" I asked.

"Just long enough to take care of the details down here."

"I'll be in touch," I said, getting up and taking a step toward her. She got up and saw me out with the briefest of amenities. She was glad to get me out of her life.

She had lied to me. But I hadn't lied to her. I *would* be in touch.

I called Judy Wise from the hotel lobby. "Judy, this is Ace Carpenter."

"Yes?" she said amiably.

"I want to know if you keep a list of the people who attend the lectures there?"

"We do, but we're not allowed to give those names out."

"I'll be right over."

I sat in the same seat I sat in the day Judy gave me the Spiritual Psychodynamics quiz. She was looking as vacuous as ever.

"Judy, were you here on Tuesday night?"

"Yes," she said sadly. "That was Mr. Smith's last lecture."

"This time around," I said cheerfully, and nodded toward the book on reincarnation that sat on the shelf next to me. That made her smile. These kids who worked in the consciousness business were like guides with no place to go—lots of signs and no destinations.

"Do you remember the girl he was talking with after the lecture?"

She thought a moment, lifting her eyes as if a replay were being run on the ceiling. Her eyes lit up. "Yes, I remember her. She was a pretty hostile individual."

"Oh?"

"She and Edward were arguing about something. In fact, they both seemed pretty upset."

"Do you know her name?"

"No. But it shouldn't be hard to find out. She was here almost a half hour before the lecture was supposed to start. Her name ought to be first on the lecture sign-in sheet."

I gave Judy a song and dance about this girl maybe being with the CIA and that I just wanted her name and address to check it out. Fanatics are the most easily manipulated people in the world.

Maureen Styles was the name at the top of the list. The next four were men's names. The address was 3945 North La Jolla Boulevard, Hollywood, California. I knew the street. It was only about ten minutes from Spiritual Psychodynamics headquarters. I thanked Judy and drove to Maureen's.

When I got there it was dusk and the house was dark. I decided to wait until I saw some activity. This was not my first stakeout. I was once hired by an old woman in Beverly Hills to look for her cat. She was obsessed with the idea that her cat had been kidnapped by another old woman a couple of blocks from her house. Personally, I thought the whole thing was pretty silly, but the hundred dollars a day made me stop laughing. I sat in my car eating egg salad sandwiches, playing solitaire, and listening to a radio station count down the top thousand songs of all time. "Satisfaction" by the Rolling Stones was first, just beating out Beethoven's *Ninth Symphony*.

Midway through the third day I found the cat. Her neighbor actually *had* kidnapped the cat in order to breed it with *her* cat. It's a crazy world. But that's OK with me. The craziness keeps me in business.

About 7:00 P.M. two cars pulled up in front of the house. One was a Mercedes, the other a Datsun 280Z. A woman dressed in tight pants and a tube top got out of the Datsun. A man in a business suit got out of the Mercedes and followed her into the house.

It was pitch dark by this time. I was dressed for skulking: black shoes, long-sleeved black shirt, and black pants; I even had a black stocking cap in the glove compartment. I got out of my car and became a slow-moving shadow. The moon was behind clouds now as I made my way silently into Maureen's backyard, a token piece of ground about as wide as a sidewalk. The house was a California stucco with brown trim around the windows and doors. I heard voices from behind a large window on my right. There were two green plastic garbage containers directly in front of the window. They were empty, so I moved them gingerly and raised my private eye to sill level.

I'll never forget what I saw as my eyes periscoped the bizarre scene. There was Maureen bedecked in dominatrix regalia: black stockings, high heels, black corset from which her rather pendulous breasts were overflowing. She stood there, riding crop in hand, above a man kneeling in his underwear looking up into Maureen's manacing gaze.

"Crawl to me, you snake," she demanded. The snake made a tiny movement toward her.

"Have you done what I told you to do?" she said to the snake.

"Yes."

"Yes, what?" she said, raising her voice ominously. Even *I* flinched a little.

"Yes, mistress," the man amended.

Maureen reminded me of Jack Webb in a movie I'd seen in which he played the part of a Marine drill instructor. Except Maureen seemed tougher.

"I always do what you say, mistress," wallowed the man further.

I wasn't sure what Maureen had asked him to do, but I was willing to bet my collection of fifties baseball cards I'd not have enjoyed doing it myself.

I walked around to the front of the house and got back in my car, where I waited for the snake to come outside. About a half hour later the guy came out. He was wearing his business suit again. He looked around, got into his car, and drove away.

I got out of my car and went to call on Maureen.

I rang the doorbell and she opened the door. She looked at me suspiciously. I tried to look at her as if I'd not just seen her playing *Fantasy Island*.

"Are you Maureen Styles?"

"Who are *you?*"

"My name is Ace Carpenter. I'm a private detective." I took out my ID and showed it to her.

She raised an eyebrow and looked coldly into my eyes. "So what do you want?"

I had a feeling I wasn't going to be asked in.

"I want to ask you a few questions about Edward Smith."

Her eyes told me she'd heard the name before and that the recall didn't hold much delight for her.

"What do ya wanna know?"

"Do you know him?"

"No." She seemed pretty certain.

I tried to jog her memory. "On Tuesday night you attended one of his lectures.

"I don't call that knowing him. I just listened to him talk."

"It seems you did some rather animated talking of your own after the lecture."

"I don't believe in what he said. I think it's copping out. Life's tough and there just ain't any easy ways around it. He tries to get people to believe there is. It's a con. I don't like it, OK?"

"It's OK with me," I said. She was a bitter young woman. It was hard to tell her age. Women like her often looked older than they were—like they were racing with time, trying to get life over with as fast as they could. "Edward Smith is dead," I said.

"So I hear. It's nothin' to me. Look, I've got to be goin'."

I didn't have any clout to make her stay and talk, so I just said, "Thanks for your time and I'll be in touch." I left her thinking about why.

On my way home I got to thinking about Kitty Jacobs. She seemed to know something she didn't want to say. If Smith were a client of Maureen's, that could be something she would want to keep quiet. A few ideas crossed my mind when I thought about Maureen and Edward Smith. Blackmail was one of them.

As I drove through Hollywood that night I began to think of it as a maze with all sorts of temptations leading off into dead ends. Most of the rats who took the cheese weren't really rats at all, but rather just run-of-the-mill mice who'd lost their way. It's easy in a maze.

Maureen reminded me of plenty of women I'd known —not necessarily in the Biblical sense—who were hard as nails and belligerent, especially toward men. I don't pretend to have figured them out, but I had a strong feeling they weren't born that way. Something had happened to them. But then, so much happens to us all. Whatever shortage is in season, there's always enough pain to go around.

* * *

Bill Jamison was the name Penny had written down when I asked her for Kathy's boyfriend's name. His over-the-garage apartment turned out to be about a mile and a half north of Sunset on Beverly Glen. A nice neighborhood; rustic, near UCLA and Bel Air. It was about 11:00 A.M. when I inquired at the front house as to whether or not I was about to knock on the right door. A woman in her mid-thirties, blonde, a little overweight, and a little bothered that I had interrupted her TV program, told me to go straight back—maybe she said something else, but I'm sure she told me to go straight somewhere. I went around back. I had decided not to call ahead. Maybe Kathy would be there, and I didn't want to scare her off.

A flight of rickety stairs led to an old wooden door with green paint peeling all over it. I knocked.

There was a slow stirring inside. I heard a door close. Then I heard the padding of bare feet approaching the door.

"You Bill Jamison?" I said.

"Who wants to know?" he replied a little defiantly. He stood there framed by the doorway, wearing white cutoff jeans, a t-shirt that depicted the signs of the zodiac from a rather sexual perspective, and a hard-ass look.

"Does who I am determine who you are?" I volleyed. The ball was in his court, but he looked as though he was familiar with the game and knew how to use a racket. I wondered how he was sizing me up.

He decided to come clean. Or at least take out a few spots to see if I'd buy it. "Yeah, yeah. I'm Bill Jamison. Who are you?"

"The name's Ace Carpenter." I removed my identification and showed it to him.

"This for real?" he muttered as he scrutinized my license.

"Nope. I just carry it for laughs. I've got a Mattel

Fanner-Fifty in the car with shootin' shells and everything. And I carry a Buck Rogers ray gun around to fend off spacemen." I landed heavily on the last word, because that's what Jamison was shaping up to be, a spaceman.

"What do you want with me? I didn't order any law to go."

I must admit I thought that was a clever thing to say and I couldn't totally hold back a grin. Through my smile I said, "I'm looking for Kathy St. John."

The name struck him like a fang. "She's not here."

"You don't mind if I come in and look around, do you?"

"I'm not having an open house, Carpenter," he said, and handed me back my ID.

"This whole matter is developing into police business. I could always call the station and get them to meet me here. Right now I don't think your card is in their deck, but I could always deal you in."

"You don't scare me," he said as if I did.

"Have it your way. I kind of like the neighborhood and I've got an hour or two to kill."

"So what do you want to know? Is Kathy here? No, she isn't. Good enough?"

"No. But then, you didn't expect it to be, did you? I'd prefer to come in and look around. I won't mess up the place and I won't look into any places too small for a person to hide." I said the latter with meaning that wasn't wasted on the young man. He might not be hiding Kathy, but a lot of people kept things in their houses that could get them free room and board in a county facility for a while.

"All right, come in. There's only one other room. Take a look and get out."

I thanked him and walked in. Besides the other room, there was a closet. I opened it and a naked woman grinned at me. She was a blonde. A natural blonde. I smiled a little while she figured out the priorities of her hand placement, finally settling on placing them on her hips and giving me a "what can I say" shrug of the shoulders.

Jamison, the gentleman at last, handed her her shoes and sat down on the bed. The blonde picked up her clothes and retired to the bathroom. As she closed the door she gave me an extra smile, which set a tingle dancing in the pit of my stomach—or lower.

"So you're Kathy's boyfriend?" I asked rhetorically.

"She's not here. You satisfied?" he said, ignoring my question.

"I am. I think Kathy might feel a little shortchanged, but then I don't write a gossip column and nobody much cares what I think. I'd like to ask you a few questions."

"What you would like doesn't concern me. Look, I let you check the place out, and you said once you did you'd go. Now get out."

His brusque manner resembled that of a Studio 54 doorman.

"I think you'll want to cooperate," I said.

"Oh? Why's that?"

"Kathy might be in trouble. She's your girlfriend, isn't she?"

"Yeah." He said it as if he were just accepting the prize for third place in a three-man race. He got off the bed, which was by now a snarl of stained sheets, and walked over to a chest of drawers. He picked up a pack of cigarettes, withdrew one, lighted it, and blew out some smoke and some tension. I heard the shower go on in the bathroom. Then a third harmony was layered onto the strained silence in the bedroom and the sound of the shower—a radio began playing a Donna Summer tune in the bathroom. I decided to take the lead vocal.

"Kathy's missing. Not for long, but it seems for certain. And she might be mixed up in something a bit dangerous. My guess is she's hiding out somewhere, confused. I could help her. In fact, that's what I'm being paid to do."

"By whom?"

"Her father."

Jamison laughed a cloud of smoke out his mouth and nostrils. "That's rich. He should have hired a private eye to find her before she took off."

"How's that?"

"Let's just say Kathy and her dad weren't close."

"Weren't?"

"Aren't. Look, if you're going to try to trip me up I won't tell you a damn thing."

"All right. Continue."

He inhaled deeply again and blew a smoke ring, and then watched it as though a drama were occurring in the round. "Yeah, well, Kathy hasn't actually lived at home for years. Some of those years I think she should have."

"What about her?"

"She thinks so, too. You ask me, I'll bet she's doing the whole prank just to get her old man to notice she's alive."

"Would she do something like that?"

"She's impulsive."

"Would she care enough about what he thinks to do it?"

"She'd say no. I'd say it's possible. You know how people are about things they know they can't have. They rationalize away the facts. The poor abstain from the evils of money. People unlucky in sex, or frustrated by the lack of it, abstain from sex and say it's bad."

"I always thought sex was a healthy aspect of life," I added a little compulsively.

"Anyhow, Kathy could have most anything she

wanted, except her old man's attention, which he channeled into other little girls, if you get my drift. So naturally, she told me and anyone else who would listen that she didn't want his attention, his fatherly love."

"Anything you can tell me about her habits?"

"She's basically pretty straight sexually."

"I mean like where she hangs out, friends, like that." I must admit that I hesitated just a little when he offered to give me the owner's manual on Kathy's sexual equipment. But work is work. Or so they say. I haven't had enough of it yet to know.

"Let's see, there's Penny Silverstein, a girl who lives in Kathy's neighborhood."

"I've talked with her."

"So you're thorough. Linda Baker. You talk with her yet?"

"Not yet. Would she have had a luncheon date with Kathy on Wednesday?" I asked, recalling the note in Kathy's appointment book.

"Can't say. Probably, though. They're real tight."

"Anyone else?"

"How about Josh?"

"I've seen the name, that's all."

"Yeah, he lives on his boat in the Marina. Name's Josh Wade. He's known Kathy since she was a little girl. He was a friend of the family's."

"Was?"

"This time you're right, was. He used to be buddies with David St. John and Kathy's mother, Ellen. I guess he was probably more of a friend of Mrs. St. John, because after Ellen died—or so Kathy tells me—Josh didn't hang around with David much anymore. But Kathy and Josh have remained friends ever since."

He took another drag off his ashing cigarette and moved across the tiny room to a chair in front of me. He still hadn't asked me to sit down. "Josh's about fifty and lives with a lady just a little younger. They're real monogamous—even though they do live in the Marina."

"Some people are just rebels," I said.

"You want to play Burns and Allen, or do you want information? You know, when Angie gets out of the shower, I'm not going to feel much like talking about Kathy. I mean, Angie's got some feelings."

"I'm sure Kathy does, too."

"That's different and you know it."

I agreed because I was short on time, not on arguments.

"When was the last time you talked with Kathy?"

"A couple days ago." He paused as if wondering if he should tell me the whole truth. "She thought I was out of town. I'm afraid I can't be too much help. Wish I could."

"I'll bet."

The shower water trickled to a drip and the music seemed louder in comparison. The door opened and Angie was nude except for a radio covering a mole on her left thigh—funny how your eye goes to places that are hidden—which was revealed when she bent down to pick up her bikini bottoms lying on the floor. She went back into the bathroom and turned the radio up a little louder. California was one hell of an interesting place. In Ohio when I was ten years old—for that matter, when I was twenty-one—I'd have considered a long-term contract with the devil to get to see what I'd just seen. Who knows, maybe I did make the deal and this was part of the payoff, and I had just forgotten about the signing.

Jamison walked toward the door and held it open as though he were getting ready to bounce me. I'm sensitive to subtleties, especially when they're not subtle. He didn't offer to see me safely to my car and I didn't wait. When I got to the curb where my VW was trying to recuperate from the drive over, I noticed a large tin garbage can. It was filled to the brim. A cloth was sticking out from under a newspaper filled with fruit cuttings. The cloth had an all-too-familiar tinge of brown spotted on it. I checked to see if Jamison could see me from his apartment. He couldn't. I pulled out the cloth. It was a sling. The kind you'd keep an injured arm in. I disturbed the woman in the front house again and called Eddy Price and told him what I'd found out.

For one thing, I'd found out Jamison was lying when he said he'd not seen Kathy. Unless, of course, she had just dropped by to put her sling in his garbage can. So Jamison was a liar. And maybe more.

But most of my thoughts centered around Kathy. I'd seen how frightened she was, how vulnerable; she was just a scared little girl yearning for the impossible safety of her mother's arms.

Eddy came down pretty hard on Jamison. It was mainly bluster, though. It was pretty clear what had happened. It was unlikely that Kathy had come to any harm and the blood—though there wasn't a great deal on the sling—was probably some of Edward Smith's and a bit from aggravating her own gunshot wound. Jamison was saying that Kathy had come to his place yesterday to tell him what was going on. And he had promised not to tell anyone where she was. That's also why he could feel so confident about having blondie over for a little afternoon delight—he knew Kathy wasn't going to drop by because it would be the first place anyone would start looking for her. So during her brief stop at Jamison's place she'd gotten rid of the bloody sling, and was off to wherever. I seriously doubted that Jamison knew where Kathy had gone. He told Eddy that Kathy had said she'd call in a few days. That made sense. If she didn't want to be found, and she knew Jamison would be asked, rather than put him in a tougher spot than he'd already be in, she probably wouldn't tell him.

Anyway, there was only so far Eddy could go. After all, Jamison hadn't committed any crime. Sins maybe, but legal infractions no. At least not anything serious. Kathy wasn't officially wanted for any crime. And it was doubtful she had met with any foul play besides her encounter with Edward Smith. Eddy knew that, but he tried to cloud the issue by constantly bringing up Smith's murder. But Jamison, though obviously put out by the inconvenience, wasn't the kind of guy to spill his guts at the drop of a hollow threat. So I left them both arguing about what each other's rights were in the situation. By the time things got down to the reading of rights, blondie had dressed, left her name with a sergeant, and split.

The Marina was about a half hour from Beverly Glen. I knew it fairly well. I liked seafood and when I felt flush I occasionally made it out to the Black Whale. Also, I used to date a girl who lived in the Oakwood Apartments in the Marina just a few blocks from the ocean. A few people who knew more about the layout of the Marina itself than I did guided me to the proper slip. I made it a habit to ask the prettiest girls I could find for directions. By doing so, I often got to where I wanted to go.

The name of the boat was the *Last Resort*. The whole Marina atmosphere was as if out of a film that might have been put together by the Marina Chamber of Commerce. The rich were playing in their king-sized tubs with their bigger-than-life toys. They were having fun, or so it seemed. The crew of the *Last Resort* consisted of one man who looked to be in his early fifties, gray hair, starting to bald, thick body, though remarkably muscular for a man his age. He wore white deck pants, a white-and-blue striped sport shirt, and tennis shoes. He was whistling while he was scraping the side of the boat with a paint-stripping tool. A woman was busily tying heavy cloth together. She appeared to be in her middle to late forties, had black hair subtly specked with gray. Her body was trim and her tanned legs were still attractive in the white shorts she was wearing. She also had on a red tube top, which ended about four inches below her bosom, allowing a relatively flat, brown tummy to show through as an obvious reminder to all that this lady was still in the game.

I was all set to ask her for directions to someplace when the man noticed me standing next to the boat.

"What can I do for ya, Mac?" he asked amiably.

"You Josh Wade?"

"That's me." He put the scraper down and moved toward me. Whatever his involvement in this affair, he was innocent. I could tell. When you approach people as an unknown quantity, and they don't know why you're there, most of them mentally scan their innermost secrets and start locking doors. You can almost hear the latches click. You can sense it in the way they shake hands, the uneasy way they smile, the too-friendly attitude, the hostile attitude. Josh Wade's bearing didn't change a degree from the time I became a question mark intruding into his safe space.

"Come on board, Mr. . . .?"

"Carpenter. Ace Carpenter."

I showed him my ID and still he reacted as if I'd just revealed that he had toes on his feet. His wife, who he introduced as Billy, had the same mellow feel about her. They led me below to a main room, which, I was told, led to three bedrooms, a galley, and a couple other rooms that I didn't quite catch. The *Last Resort* seemed large enough to have its own ballroom.

I was offered—and accepted—a highball and finger

sandwiches. Over the snack I told them pretty much all of what had gone down and that I would appreciate anything they could tell me about how I might be able to locate Kathy St. John. The two of them seemed genuinely concerned about Kathy's welfare.

"She and Bill were here last weekend. They generally spend at least one of the weekend days out here with us," said Billy.

"They were here with us Sunday. We went over to Catalina, if I recall," said Wade.

"Is there anyone besides you two and Jamison whom she might contact?"

"She has other friends, of course," said Wade. "But Bill and the two of us are her closest friends."

"Has she ever taken off without telling anyone before?"

"She is impulsive. But, she never worries her close friends. You might say Billy and I are Kathy's substitute parents. She's spent more time with us over the past ten years than with her father by a considerable margin."

"I keep hearing about ten years ago," I said. "That's when Mrs. St. John was killed, right?"

"That's correct," said Wade.

"Could you tell me a little bit about the St. John family? It's all coming to me in jigsaw puzzle pieces."

"We were good friends of David and Ellen—that's Mrs. St. John. We knew them in the middle fifties before Kathy was born, when I was just beginning to make money as a lawyer," explained Wade. "David and I knew each other from law school. Billy and Ellen got on quite well, also—even though they were really about 180 degrees apart in personality."

"How so?" I asked, munching down on a piece of salami.

"There's no use in being subtle," Wade's wife replied. "If you're trying to get an overview of the St. John family, the truth is the only thing that'll do you any good," said Billy, seemingly invigorated at the memory and the opportunity to retell it.

"I don't know what you know about Ellen, but she was from a very wealthy family in Pasadena. Her father had owned a great deal of the Valley in the early part of the century and had been wise enough to hold onto it until it could provide enough money to make him financially independent for a number of lifetimes."

"Some of those lifetimes were used up at a breakneck pace by his daughter, Ellen," added Wade.

Then his wife picked up the story again. "David was a bright light on the law scene back then, and he was ambitious. Marrying Ellen virtually assured the attainment of most of the material goals he'd set for himself."

"I was a good friend of his, and I honestly don't know if he had any other kind of goal," said Wade, draining the last of his highball, rising, and going to the bar to fix himself another. He asked if I needed a refill. I asked what the date was. He said a number. It was odd and I told him I had even license plates and that I was doing my best to ration. He laughed and fixed himself another highball.

"The marriage was a fair exchange," continued Billy. "Ellen got a handsome, intelligent, power-hungry man who fit into her picture of the man who would stand beside her in all the family pictures. And David got the security, the connections by association, and the credibility he needed to build a phenomenally successful practice.

"But it was all a facade. David was power mad and had little time for domestic demands unless there was some carrot at the end of the stick. Ellen, on the other hand, now with built-in respectability, was free to do whatever she pleased."

"What pleased her was other men," said Wade, rejoining his wife and me.

"She was loose?"

"Yes is the most understated way to say it," said Billy. "When Kathy came along, the child was just another fixture on their mantlepiece to be collectively presented as a picture of familial tranquility. From the time she was born, Kathy was usually under the supervision, if not outright care, of hired nurses and babysitters. David's participation in Kathy's upbringing was almost nonexistent. And Ellen's contribution was the scheduling and paying of hired help to take care of Kathy. When Ellen died, David simply sent Kathy away to school most of the time to remove her distracting influence from his otherwise orderly daily routine."

"He had faith that money would buy her what he wasn't willing to give," continued Wade. "It didn't, of course. It never does. We started taking Kathy on vacations when she'd come home to—L.A. and David wouldn't spent time with her."

"What about Ellen's death?" I asked.

"A skiing accident. Happened in Zurich," said Wade.

"How did Kathy take it?" I asked.

"Pretty well. It was kind of like losing someone you knew, but weren't too close to," said Billy, sipping at her highball.

"So why would David St. John be so upset and anxious about his daughter's disappearance now?"

"I don't know," said Wade. "Maybe because it's the expected thing to do. David's big on protocol. I imagine that it seems the most logical, acceptable way to act."

"But he seemed truly upset," I prodded.

"Can't say why David acts the way he does," said Billy. "He's a tough man to figure out."

"You and Josh see much of David St. John anymore?"

"Never. We haven't seen David socially for about a decade now."

"It seems the turning point in a lot of lives was Ellen's death," I observed.

We talked a bit more, they took my card and promised to call me if they heard from Kathy. Not to turn her in, but just to let David know she was all right.

When I stepped off the yacht I felt as though I were stepping off a million dollar bill. If there were such a thing, it would probably look and feel like the Wade's boat felt to me.

It was early evening by the time I got back from the Marina. It was warm enough to eat my grilled cheese sandwich and sip a medium-priced wine on my patio. I put my feet up on the railing and watched an orange moon explode in slow motion behind a hill. It cleared to a full bright white as it began to course the silhouetted L.A. skyline. It was like a bouncing ball in a singalong song except that it never dipped low enough to touch any of the words. It was as if Hollywood tonight was a song without words, a sad song.

"Hello."

"Linda?"

"Yes. Who's this?"

"My name's Carpenter. Ace Carpenter. I'm a friend of Kathy St. John's. I'm a private detective hired by her father to find her. I'd like to come by and talk to you for a few minutes if I could."

"What about?"

"I'd rather discuss it in person."

"How do I know you're who you say you are?"

"When's the last time someone called you and lied to you about being a detective?"

She thought a minute. "Never."

"Well, there you go. Even if I'm not on the level, I'm creative."

She laughed.

"OK, but I've been having some trouble with my car lately. I just got it back from the garage. I'd like to drive it. So I'll meet you somewhere for coffee."

She still didn't trust me. She didn't want me knowing

where she lived. That was OK with me. After all, I just wanted to ask her some questions.

"All right. Where do you live?"

"Culver City. Where are you now?"

"Hollywood," I said.

"I'll meet you some place in Hollywood."

"OK. How about Figaro's on Melrose?"

"I know where that is."

"An hour from now?"

"OK. I'm blonde and I'll be wearing a black velvet coat and jeans."

* * *

A blonde-haired, green-eyed woman, in her early twenties sat in the corner of Figaro's. She was wearing a black velvet jacket and jeans. She looked up and waved me over. I sat down, introduced myself, and ordered an Oktoberfest Malt. I drink a little, but I had to admit that two of those made me feel like dancing with fire hydrants.

Linda seemed like a nice girl. Sounds like an overworked phrase, but she was the kind of girl who probably originally inspired the line. She smiled a lot, smoked as much, and made her lightly made-up eyes larger when she listened to me, as though she really wanted to hear what I had to say. I wasn't used to people giving me all their attention when I talked, so, at first, I had to try extra-hard to be coherent. Not that I'm not usually, just that I was on my guard.

"Is Kathy in some kind of trouble?" she asked, flicking an ash into the ashtray that I'd had her move to one side of the table. I don't like smoke blowing in my face.

"No. At least I don't think so. I'm just concerned."

All I went on to tell Linda was that Kathy's father had hired me to find his daughter because she had disappeared. I skipped the juicy parts.

"As a matter of fact, we were supposed to meet at two at Butterfield's on Wednesday, but she called that morning and said she'd have to change it to noon. When I arrived at Butterfield's she was already there. She was upset about something."

"Did she say what it was?"

"No. And I didn't ask. Kathy and I've been friends for about five years. We both know when to ask questions and when not to."

"You say you've been friends with Kathy for about five years."

"I'm a stewardess for Pan Am. I met her when she was coming back from New York about five years ago. We struck up a conversation. She's into jazz and collecting art. So am I. We started going to museums together and double-dating. You know."

I didn't know, really, but I said I did. I haven't been friends with anybody for that long except a secretary at a finance company. And I had my reasons. I've been called a manipulator. I prefer the title survivor. Probably neither one of them is 100 percent accurate. But I have the feeling there's more than a little truth in both.

"Did she say anything, give you any indication she might be going away for a while?"

"No."

Just then a waitress with a little smock, a broad smile, a tiny waist, and large breasts arrived with my Oktoberfest and Linda's gin and tonic, which she must have ordered before I came in. The waitress departed quickly and I resumed my dialogue with the stewardess.

"Tell me a little about Kathy," I said. "What's she like?"

"How do I know you're who you say you are? Do you have some identification?"

I took out my ID, which seemed to do the trick. I was always amazed at how willing people were to accept a piece of paper that could so easily be forged. I was thinking of buying a pipe and having some identification printed up that said I was Hugh Hefner.

"Kathy is a very nice girl. She comes from a well-known family." I noticed she didn't say a good family. "She's generous, impulsive."

"Impulsive? How so?"

"She'd see things she wanted, or wanted to do; like skiing, for instance. Two years ago Kathy met a guy who was into skiing. The very next day she went down to the Big Five Sporting Goods store and got outfitted in the best ski equipment available and signed up for skiing lessons. By the next weekend she was on the slopes. By the following weekend, she had said good-bye to the ski enthusiast, packed her ski gear in mothballs, and was taking tennis lessons from some Pancho Gonzales-type in Palm Springs. She hasn't touched the skiing equipment since. That's just a typical example. It happens all the time."

"Does she ever stick to anything?"

"She collects art. She's done that as long as I've known her. Tell you the truth, it's kind of surprising."

"What is?"

"Well, it isn't like she knows a great deal about it. She just likes the scene. She seems to live vicariously through the artists she meets. Most of them are starving anyhow and are quite impressed that someone with money—someone as good-looking as Kathy—would take the time to get to know them. It's an exchange of needs, desires. Each has a hunk of what the other needs to survive. The artist needs recognition, success, money, and often adoration—maybe to make up for the condescension he gets until success comes. And Kathy needs to believe she has more value than just having money and being a sex object. It's kind of funny."

"What?"

"Oh, nothing."

"Come on now. What's funny?"

"Well, it's like the whole thing is such a farce. By Kathy deciding to give her attention and money to an artist, she thereby legitimizes his art. By him returning the attention in terms of raising her to patron status, she is made credible, valuable. The mutual success is therefore manufactured. The artist isn't necessarily good, and she isn't necessarily sincere. Doesn't that seem kind of unfair to you? I mean, Kathy might just want to get in bed with some guy who paints worth shit and all of a sudden the whole scene becomes legitimate with her money and connections. Kind of strange, if you ask me," she said, revealing an undercurrent of bitterness.

"It sounds as though a renaissance could flourish again if Kathy St. John were a little more promiscuous."

"I didn't mean to imply that Kathy was promiscuous. She's not."

Though Linda mouthed the words, it sounded as though they would crack if I bit into them hard. I decided to save that snack for another time.

"I understand. She's not promiscuous. She's liberated. I didn't drive over here in a covered wagon. Tell me about Kathy's boyfriend."

"Bill Jamison. He lives near UCLA."

"An artist who made it?" I decided not to mention my meeting with Jamison.

"No," she said, sipping her drink and stubbing out the remnants of her Dunhill in the ashtray. "He lives over the garage of a house. He's an up-and-coming artist, though."

"Aren't they all?" I said, swishing the remaining third of my brew in the frosted mug. "How long has she been with Bill?"

"About a year. That's a long time for Kathy. I personally think she's serious."

"Sincere would be more to my liking, but then she's not my girl."

"They're very close. I'm sure if you're having difficulty finding Kathy, Bill would know. If anyone would."

Linda and I talked a little while longer, though not much about Kathy. Linda was an interesting conversationalist. We liked a few of the same things: baseball, reading, and public television. I made a mental note to call her later.

I used a phone booth outside Figaro's to call Eddy at the West Hollywood Station. I asked him if he could get away for a few minutes. He could. I met him at the Yamashiro for a drink and a double shot of the view from the top of the mountain. I always liked the Yamashiro. First of all, I have a predilection for the Oriental way of life. Especially the women. Secondly, I love views. And the Yamashiro had one of the best in town.

Eddy stumbled in about eleven and found his way to where I was working on a Stolichnaya. He ordered a cup of coffee and we commented on how the Santa Ana winds had made the city nearly visible again.

"Anything new on the St. John case?" I asked finally.

"A couple of things," said Eddy, sipping from his recently delivered cup. "I think we've got a witness to the Old World shooting. A dishwasher at a restaurant, the Kazkav, across the street from the Old World. It's a Russian place. Never been there. Have you?"

"Once. I'm not much for Russian food. Vodka, yes."

"So anyhow, it seems this guy, Tim Warden's his name, was dumping some garbage out back when he heard a shot. He saw a man running with a rifle in his hands. The alleged assailant," said Eddy, as if he were reading from his notebook, "then got into a late model American-made car—most likely a black Trans-Am according to the description—and sped away."

"Hmmm," I hummed, as I digested the information as well as another sip of vodka. "How good a look at the guy did Warden get?"

"Warden is sure the guy with the rifle was Oriental. As far as whether he was Japanese, Chinese, whatever, he couldn't tell."

"Any license number?"

"Nope. But it was a California plate. It seems Warden did a good job of concealing himself as fast as he could when he saw the rifle."

"Understandable. Mind if I talk with him?"

"No. Not as long as he's willing to talk with you. We're through with him. Give him ten dollars and he'll probably be willing to put it on tape."

"Eight-track or cassette?"

"I don't . . . That's cute," said Eddy with a grin, and tipped his cup to me as he guided it up to his lips.

"What about Jamison?"

"Nothing. Kathy was there, but, as I'm sure you figured, he doesn't know where the hell she is now. I believe him, but he's kind of a punk, this Jamison."

"Yeah, he is. Anything else?"

"Not much. St. John hasn't officially filed a missing persons report. So finding her—at least right now—is still your responsibility. Officially. Of course, we would like to talk with her because of her involvement with the now deceased Edward Smith. Obviously she didn't kill him, but we'd like to talk with her to see what she knows. But from what you tell me, it sounds as if she doesn't know too much."

"She might have gotten an education in the past twenty-four hours," I said. "What do you know about David St. John?"

"Not much," said Eddy, draining his cup and stopping the very Oriental waitress who was passing by. He ordered another java. "He's a lawyer. Showbiz lawyer. Handles some of the biggies. Worth a few million, I guess."

"That explains the pictures I saw on the walls."

"What pictures?"

"Pictures of himself with a virtual who's who of L.A.'s film and political elite. What about St. John and his daughter? Good relationship?"

"Hard to tell. I just got on the case, Ace. But from what we can tell, she hasn't really lived at home for about ten years."

"Which would make it since she was about eleven. I'm curious about something. It's probably way off base, but see if you can find out something about the death of St. John's wife."

"Why?"

"Her death corresponds approximately to the time that a whole lot of things started going sour. I'm just curious. If you could get me some of the basics, I'll run with it, do the digging, and give you what I come up with."

"Fair enough."

It was about one in the morning when I arrived at the Kit Kat Club on Melrose near Vine. Teddy, the guy at the door, smiled and let me pass without cover. The Kit Kat was a strip joint. Classy, though. After most of the bottomless clubs were closed in the early seventies, just a few clubs hung on. The girls in these special few were dynamite. I'd been turned on to the place after I'd done a recording session down the street a couple of years ago. I'd played guitar on a demo for a friend. He ended up cutting an album and bedding fourteen-year-old groupies. I ended up tracking down missing persons and having Jenny Ling as a friend.

Jenny was about five feet two in high heels, which she wore for her number. She had been known to wear them elsewhere. In bed, for example. She had a nice tan and string bikini marks that were clearly visible during her act, which she was doing right now. She spotted me as I sat down. I ordered a Stolichnaya and put a dollar bill over the piece of string that surrounded the stage. She came over, picked up the bill, and did something special just for me.

After she finished, she put on her bikini bottom and

a halter top and came over and sat down. I didn't have
to buy her drinks. We were friends and more than occasional lovers. In fact, she sometimes bought me drinks.

"Business or pleasure?" she said, crossing her slim,
naked legs.

"You know that separating pleasure from seeing you
is like trying to take print off a page."

She liked that. We always had a good time together.
Usually we went to see detective films. I was the closest
thing she could find to Phillip Marlowe. She was the
closest thing I could find to an honest woman.

"You know anything about the kinky sex scene in
L.A.? S & M stuff?"

"A little. It's not my bag. Except for the little thing
you already know about."

I smiled, like I'd just remembered where I lost something valuable.

"I met a woman named Maureen Styles who's a real
whip wielder. You know how I could find out something
about her?"

"I've got a few friends who work S & M outcalls.
Sometimes the girls know each other, or at least hear
about each other."

"Maureen Styles. See if anyone's heard of her," I said,
tasting my drink, which had just been delivered.

"Anything in it for the girl if she knows something?"

"They take Master Charge nowadays, don't they?"

"Uh huh."

"Then I'll see what I can do. I'm working these days."

"What about tonight?" she said, playfully bouncing
one calf off her crossed knee. She smiled and her almond
eyes became one exciting sensation aimed at me full
strength.

"I get off about now," I said, looking at my watch.

"I get off in an hour. Let's both get off a little later."

No negative arguments came to mind and any that

tried to were melted away from the heat that had electrified my body.

"You're on," I said.

She smiled a little wider, a little more wickedly, got up, and moved her Asian body through the sensuous paces she was paid to perform for the lonely men who stationed themselves near the stage and the fantasy that danced upon it. It was late enough so that most of the guys there knew that a look was all they were going to get tonight. They would take a strong visual impression home to bed with them and try to nurse some comfort out of it. Me, I was going home with Jenny Ling. And she didn't need any coaxing.

On the way over to Jenny's we passed an all-night stuffed animal stand at the corner of Highland and Sunset. The guy in charge looked like a carnival vendor waiting to hand out prizes. At two in the morning, even Sunset Boulevard looked empty and the only people left walking the streets didn't look like winners.

The next morning I awoke revitalized and refreshed. Nights with Jenny had a tendency to have that effect on me. It was about 9:30 by the time I got dressed and coffeed. I kissed my sleeping Asian beauty and silently left her place and went home.

After a shower and an omelette I called St. John and told him I thought it would be a good idea if we got together. He suggested lunch. I agreed. His house at 11:30. As soon as I hung up I noticed my glass of orange juice start to wiggle slightly on the coffee table. Then it stopped. Just another earthquake. I had become complacent in the presence of acts of God.

Through the trembling earth, which occasionally rearranged door frames and freeway overpasses, the sounds of depression, chaos, and an imminent violent decade could be sensed everywhere, in everything, in the late seventies. In Hollywood, that feeling of helpless frustra-

tion was often transmuted into less-severely punished
forms of behavior. Flamboyancy was a type, though an
impotent one, of civil disobedience. Hollywood was the
"self" capital of the world. A place where starvation and
pestilence were just salt and pepper spicings for a good
script, things people could understand only in terms of
celluloid magnified by light. A mass killing? Great stuff
for a TV movie, but move fast because the public is del-
uged with so much terror they might forget. A famous
person slain? Excellent. Who will we get? Redford?
Hoffman? What about Pacino? Or even Brando himself!
A child is killed in a hit and run. No, no, too small.
Maybe for a minor theme on a half hour situation com-
edy; something for contrast. The public needs more sensation.

It all seemed like a mirage then. Images without sub-
stance. Causes without commitment. Sex without feeling. And still I called Hollywood home. But it was like
waiting for the other shoe of a hostile giant to fall. So I
kept busy. We all did.

St. John answered the door himself. He didn't have a
flower in his lapel today. He was dressed casually in
white trousers and a sport shirt. He led me into the living room and we sat down. There were two glasses of
orange juice sitting on the table between us. One was
mine.

I got right to the point. "Mr. St. John, as you know
I've been making inquiries into your daughter's disappearance. So far neither I nor the police have come up
with anything. Have you heard from her?"

"No. And I don't expect to. At least not right away."
I detected a note of strained tolerance in his voice.

"Has this happened before?"

"Let's just say that my daughter does not concern
herself with giving me a detailed report of her comings
and goings."

"Is that a long yes?"

"Yes," he said as if it were a little distressing for him to do anything I told him to do. Even give me an answer.

From where I was sitting I could see St. John's pool, and beyond that the city of L.A. The perpetual brown blanket of smog was tucking the city in for another hazy day. Between the city and myself a young girl, who wouldn't have had a prayer of being allowed into an R-rated movie by herself for at least a couple of years, danced past the window wearing the briefest of bikini bottoms and dove into the water. She wore nothing on top, but even the most cursory of observations indicated that if for no other reason than the law of gravity, she ought to don some type of supporting equipment.

St. John tried not to notice. He tried hard. I didn't mention it, but the silence made my point.

"I've talked with some friends of yours," I said finally.

"Oh? Who?" he asked, raising his glass of juice to his lips and giving me a questioning frown. I think he was surprised to hear the news he had any friends. I was prepared to let him down easy.

"Josh Wade."

"I see," he said. I'm sure he did. What he didn't see was a friend. "We're actually not close anymore. But I'm sure you know that if you talked with him about me."

"Yeah, well, he said he used to be friends with the whole family. Way back. Before your wife died."

"I think Josh was more a friend of my wife's than of mine."

"He tells me you two went to law school together."

"That's true. But as my practice began to grow, my past acquaintances began to fade measurably from my sphere of activity."

"But not from your wife's."

"I trust that you are not hinting at something unsavory, Mr. Carpenter. The facts are simple. My wife was a very social person. She could not stand to be alone. All of *our* friends virtually became hers as demands on my time increased."

"You and your wife were very different people," I said, trying to keep my attention on the conversation as the nymph outside pulled herself out of the pool and padded animatedly to the diving board. Her breasts arrived at the board shortly before the rest of her. I continued to watch her out of the corner of my eye.

"Our differences were what made us so compatible. We complemented each other. We weren't carbon copies of each other. It worked out well for the time we had together."

"Why does Kathy still see so much of Josh Wade?"

St. John started to say something, but decided not to. I think I genuinely surprised him. It wasn't a pleasant surprise either. "To be quite honest with you, Mr. Carpenter, I was not aware that my daughter was seeing Josh Wade."

"From what her boyfriend and the Wades tell me, she usually spends one of the weekend days each week on Wade's yacht."

"What boyfriend!" said St. John, both in disgust and in an attempt to veer the conversation a little from an area in which he felt uncomfortable. "This Jamison boy is a loser. But then, I haven't exactly agreed with my daughter's taste in companions for quite some time. Maybe never."

"You've met Jamison?"

"He burst in one night while my daughter and I were having dinner together at the California Club. A low life, if you ask me. He wasn't dressed for the place, for one thing. Probably couldn't dress for it even if he *knew* what was required. Anyhow, he was admitted because he used my name with the maitre d'. My name!" said St. John, as if someone with leprosy had just drunk from his glass. "My daughter, in her ignorance, had made the mistake of telling this young man where we were dining and he took it as an invitation. I do not mind telling you I was humiliated. Jamison's manner was rude, disrespectful, and visibly unrefined."

I straightened the collar of my shirt and contemplated calling him sir after the dissertation. I decided against it, not wanting to place myself any lower on the social ladder in relationship to St. John than I already felt. As it was, I felt about eye-level with the first rung.

"You want to tell me anything else about Josh Wade? It seems Kathy and he were close. I'm trying to find her and I need all the help I can get."

"Obviously, since I have not remained in touch with the Wades over the years and I find it surprising that my daughter is still in contact with them, there is not a great deal I can say. Certainly nothing to shed any light on this current matter."

"Why did you stop seeing the Wades after your wife died?"

"I told you it was a gradual thing."

"You said while your wife was alive, she took over more of the social obligations. Wade says that since her death you haven't seen each other at all. Doesn't that seem strange to you? I'm just a private eye, but it seems strange to me. If you all were friends, it would seem that there would be some kind of bond, at least enough so that you'd stay in touch—send Christmas cards, things like that."

"I don't imagine it occurred to you that after my wife's death I would want to cut all ties with the past that reminded me of her. It was an extremely difficult time for me. I don't say that to evoke sympathy."

He didn't have to say that. It didn't.

"I loved my wife very much. We did not spend every waking moment together, but in our own way we loved each other. It has taken me a long time to get over her death. In some ways, I guess I will never totally get over it."

I heard the speech, heard the words. But St. John didn't look like the kind of guy who experienced much pain. He was the kind of guy who sent his pain out to be laundered and it came back anger or some other more pragmatic emotional color.

St. John was not ready to talk about his past. At least not now. I debated whether or not to ask him about what the Wades had said about his wife playing around. I decided against it. I'd play that card when it could win a bigger pot.

Just then the topless teenager opened the glass doors and, drying herself as she entered, came in and sat down next to St. John.

"You are dripping water on the furniture," he said, raising his voice irritably. "Use a little common sense." I had the feeling he wasn't just talking about getting the furniture wet.

The girl jumped up from the chair in which she was sitting. "I'm sorry," she said in a high, timid voice. "I'll wipe it with this towel." She started to do just that.

"Use the towel to cover yourself, for chrissakes. We're not alone, in case you didn't notice," he said, tilting his head in my direction.

The girl smiled and wrapped the towel around her breasts. "My name's Jennifer."

"My name's Ace. Glad to meet you." I was *more* glad when she wasn't wearing her towel, but I thought it would be in bad taste if I asked her to take it off again.

"If we're all done playing show and tell and exchanging names," said St. John, "I think that is all we have to discuss, Mr. Carpenter."

St. John rolled his eyes a little and rubbed his forehead as if trying to keep the pain at bay and having trouble doing so.

"Oh, by the way, what kind of car does your house-boy drive?" I asked as I rose.

"That's a strange question."

"Humor me."

"A red Toyota."

"All right. I'll call you soon and let you know how the case is coming," I said.

I said my good-byes and let myself out. It must have been St. John's houseboy's day off.

I went to the first phone booth I could find at the bottom of the hill. It was at a motel across the street from the Old World Restaurant. I called the San Francisco number I'd gotten from Kathy St. John's apartment.

"Hello," I said.

"Yes. Who is this?" It was a woman's voice.

"Who is this?" I asked. "I'm calling the Phillip Schneider residence in San Francisco."

"This is a Sausalito residence. You have the wrong number."

"But Sausalito's near San Francisco, isn't it?" I continued.

"Certainly, but you have the wrong number. This is not the Schneider residence. This is th . . ."

"Yes? Who do I have on the line?"

"Who *is* this?" She became alarmed.

"I'm a friend of Kathy St. John's and . . ."

The line went dead. I didn't know who I had on the line, but whoever it was seemed to know who Kathy St. John was and wasn't in the mood to talk about her.

I drove up the winding road that led to the hills near the Hollywood sign and my home. I called my answering service. Jenny had called. "That was all," said the answering service girl. I sensed an editorial comment in her remark.

I called Eddy and asked him to meet me at the Brassiere for a drink about six if he could make it. He could. I called Jenny and she said she had a friend who knew Maureen Styles. I thanked Jenny, called her friend, asked if she accepted Master Charge, and set a late afternoon appointment. I had about three hours to kill, so I settled down to a little Ludlum and fell asleep as some guy was getting garroted in a country I'd never heard of.

I was awakened about four-thirty by the doorbell. A brunette, about five-feet-three, with shoulder-length hair, lots of makeup, a green dress with a thigh-high slit up one side, no stockings, brown high heels, and a smile stood at my door.

"So you're Ace Carpenter," she said, as if she knew something humorous about me. Jenny wasn't always discreet.

"Uh huh. You Jenny's friend?"

"That's right."

"Come on in."

She did and I motioned for her to sit on my davenport. The view of the city was nice from there and always made a good impression on first-timers. She was impressed and said so.

"Something to drink?" I asked from the kitchenette area. "Got juice, orange and apple, water, Diet Pepsi, and some Stolichnaya."

"Orange juice," she said, settling into a comfortable position on the sofa by tucking one trim, toned leg up under the other.

I brought some juice for both of us into the living room, handed her a glass, and sat down opposite her.

"So what's your name?" I asked, sipping my citrus.

"Tammy. Tammy Southern." It sounded like a name you'd give a john, but it wasn't necessary to get nosy with her.

"So, Tammy, I guess Jenny told you that I wanted to get some information about Maureen Styles."

"Yeah. She says you're a private detective."

"Most of the time."

"What do you do the rest of the time?" she asked, obviously taking me literally.

"I ride in a rodeo."

"No kidding." She seemed impressed. In fact, she seemed so impressed that I decided not to tell her I was lying.

"So how do you know Maureen Styles?"

"We used to work at the same massage parlor over on Hollywood Boulevard near La Brea."

"When was this?"

"About two years ago."

"Do you know anything about her activities in the sadomasochistic scene?"

"Yeah. About two years ago, the massage parlor I was workin' at was having trouble making ends meet. So the manager decided to hang another sign out front. Instead of callin' it the Pussycat Palace of Delights, it was called the Leather Palace. Any of the girls who wanted to switch to that scene could stay. They could make about twice the money they were makin' before. Anyhow, this brought the crazies out of the woodwork. The girls comin' in looking for work were usually just tryin' to make a buck any way they could. But Maureen was different. She was really into the scene."

"Were you and Maureen friends?"

"Not quite friends. A little more than acquaintances, though. We'd spend most of the sittin' time—you know, when nothin' was happenin'—talkin' to each other. She didn't open up easy, but I could tell from what she *did* say, she was one unhappy lady."

"How so?" I asked, sipping a little harder on my juice.

"She said her mother was an alcoholic. Her father died when she was young. I think she was takin' care of her mother. That's one reason she needed so much money. Maureen had a lot of hate in her, but she wasn't a bad girl."

"How do you mean?"

"In the business, you get a feel for bad. Now I met people, bad people, who'd do you dirty for the price of a bottle of wine. No such thing as loyalty to nothin'. Maureen hated, but she didn't hate blindly. Something had happened to her. She was fair, if not kind, to all the people she worked with, and I hardly ever heard her talk bad behind anyone's back."

"What did Maureen hate?"

"She'd never really say. That part of her was private. Whatever it was, it burned like a fire inside her. It kept her goin'. Maybe she was ashamed to show it. Maybe she thought if she showed it to anyone, it'd disappear and she'd run down."

"You say she really liked S & M. What in particular?"

"Humiliatin' men."

"Anything else you can think of that might be of help?"

She hesitated and sipped at her juice. There was something else, and I hoped she'd decide to say it.

"I told Jenny this and she thought it might be important. But I feel kind of like a snitch tellin' you. After all, we were friends."

"I'm not digging into Maureen's past to blackmail her or anything. A young woman's life may be at stake and I'm just trying to get a handle on the personalities involved. Anything you tell me will be treated with discretion."

"OK. There was something she did with her regular customers that was kind of kinky. She used to have this ID bracelet with the initials E. M. on it. She'd make her customers wear it while she humiliated them."

"How do you know?"

"Occasionally I'd come in and watch. Some guys like that, ya know."

I didn't, but I nodded as if she'd just told me breathing was healthy.

"That's interesting. You know what the letters E. M. stand for?"

"No. The way I figured it, they were probably the initials of some guy who'd given her a bad time."

"Seems logical. But you said you never saw her with any guy."

"Like I say, we were acquaintances at work. We didn't socialize."

There was a moment or two of silence. I was thinking about what, if anything, this information meant, while Tammy was probably wondering whether or not she'd done the right thing in telling me.

"So when was the last time you saw Maureen?"

"About nine months ago. I heard she went into business for herself. She was always talkin' about doing that, so I guess she did. Anyhow, she quit the Leather Palace."

"And you haven't seen each other since?"

"No."

"Did she have any customer who was more regular than any other?"

"You mean someone who came all the time to see her, then didn't come anymore after she left?"

"Uh huh."

"There was one guy. He was devoted to Maureen. He'd come in three, four, sometimes five times a week."

"He'd have to have some money to do that, wouldn't he?"

"Damn right. Thirty-five dollars a pop, minimum."

"You know the guy's name?"

"No. They never give their real names anyhow. After Maureen quit, he stopped comin'. I doubt if his interest waned. I figure she could make a nice livin' off of just him."

"What did he look like?"

"Good-looking guy. About thirty-five, forty. Just a

little under six feet, sandy hair, lean, well-built. Always came in well-dressed."

It sounded a lot like the guy I'd seen at Maureen's place the night before. I drained my juice, raised my eyebrows, and smiled at Tammy. "Well, that's about it. Thanks. I'll give you your thirty-five dollars for a half hour. That's right, isn't it?"

"Yes, but we haven't done anything."

"We've done what I asked you to come here to do. I needed information, you gave it to me. Besides, the thirty-five is part of my expenses. It doesn't come out of my pocket."

"I just thought you might want to, uh . . ."

"Yeah, well, maybe another time, when you're off duty."

She said sure, gave me her home phone, and gladly accepted the thirty-five.

The atmosphere of the Brassiere was beginning to congeal, as it did each night about this time. The actors, writers, would-be anything glamorous were taking up their positions on a paint-by-number drawing. Though each had a specific hue and tone, together they always formed a portrait of oblivious desperation. The overall effect was ambiguity not unlike the famous painting that, when looked at from various perspectives, appeared to be alternately smiling and sad. My fellow Brassiere regulars were used to laughing in a most sad manner.

It was dark by five-thirty these days, so a lot of people didn't feel real self-conscious about drinking a little earlier than usual. I ordered a Stolichnaya and waited for Eddy. While I waited I overheard two guys talking about doing voice-overs for commercials. One guy was saying he really liked the other guy's voice. They both started talking about the one guy's voice as though it were another person. The guy with the voice said his girlfriend's hands were involved in two different dish-washing soap commercials. They both agreed that she had the best hands they'd ever seen. The guy with the average, run-of-the-mill talking voice was saying that he was trying to get his hips into some ads for the May Company. Apparently they weren't interested in his up-per body, just his hips. I'd seen ads like that a million times and I've never looked at another one quite the same since.

They talked on and on about trying to get different parts of their bodies into advertisements. I think the only body parts they didn't consider pushing were their brains. But then, I didn't really think either would have any serious offers. Besides, mindlessness is the basic building block of advertising. And these guys sitting next to me were probably giants in the field. At least part of a giant.

Eddy arrived a little after six, ordered a beer, and sat down. He made a few noises about what a tough day he'd had. I was all ears. Hell, maybe I could rent my ears to the telephone company for a commercial.

"Anything new on the Smith murder?"

"Nope. Haven't located the Oriental gunman, but we're working on it. Besides that, Smith didn't have any warrants out for his arrest. He's clean with the IRS, his bills are paid. What can I tell ya? He might have been straight."

"Didn't know you were into religion, Eddy," I said.

"I didn't say we'd be close. There are a lot of guys who are nice that aren't my friends. And some who aren't so nice—like you," he smiled, "who are."

I sipped at my drink and sat silently for a moment. In the background I heard something about a foot and an ankle.

"You get anything on St. John's wife's death?"

That brightened Eddy up a little. "I did. Just the seed

of something, though. You're gonna have to water it and see if it grows."

"Fine with me. Whatcha got?"

He took out his notebook and leafed through some pages. "Here it is." He tore out a page and laid it in front of me. "Guy's name is Everett Gray. He was a writer for the *Times* when Ellen St. John was killed. Since then he's switched over to the *Herald-Examiner*. When Ellen St. John was killed he did a long article on how she died, what she'd done for the community—you know, all the obligatory things you say about people when it's too late for them to hear and too dead for anyone to mind the exaggerations. Anyhow, he's your man. The article sounds as though he knew the family pretty well. I guess the St. Johns were one big deal a few years back."

I folded the paper and tucked it away in a pocket. Gray sounded like an easy guy to locate. If he were willing to talk, I might come away with a lot of answers and most likely some fascinating, tough questions.

"You know anything about Gray that'd be helpful?" I asked.

"The guy who got the information for me said Gray drinks a little too much—probably not as much as you —and plays the horses in a not-too-smart way. He's divorced. About seven years ago. His only record is for disturbing the peace back in '74."

"How'd that happen?"

"Arrested for marching in a gay rights parade. There was a scuffle with a group of construction workers and, well, you know the story. The guy's actually pretty clean. I mean, we don't have any orders to shoot to kill."

"Thanks, Eddy. I've just got a hunch about this. It might not prove out, but this lead ought to go a long way toward proving whether or not I'm on a hot scent."

"What do you have goin' for tonight?" Eddy asked.
"I'm working."
"Yeah, well, you know you work a lot at night."
"Criminals are lazy. They sleep all day."

I liked Hollywood at night. It was like one strained allegory come to life. Or as near to life as it was going to get. The flashy, trashy billboards, the flashy, trashy women, the flickering lights dotting the haze-hidden hills, the cars, the movement, the gaiety, and the despair. Whatever else it was, it wasn't boring.

I'd never been to the California Club before. It was a nice place to be overcharged. I made my way to the bar and ordered a Stolichnaya. The bartender was a guy from Scotland. He had quite a sense of humor. It made me like the place more. We struck up an amiable conversation. He used to play in a rock 'n' roll band that was once on the same bill with the Beatles and Led Zeppelin in England. Now that was as good as smearing blood on each other's thumbs as far as I was concerned. We launched into a meaningful dialogue on the effect of British music, yesterday and today, on American popular music.

I told him I was a private detective and showed him my ID. The ID made an impression, the name made him laugh. His name was Stephen. It was all right, but not as funny as mine.

"So you're working for David St. John?"

"Uh huh. He said he and his daughter had dinner here last Tuesday night." I showed him the picture I had of Kathy.

"Yeah, they were in," said Stephen. "David eats here a couple times a week. He just lives a few minutes from here up on Blue Jay Way."

The mention of Blue Jay Way got us off on a tangent about the Beatles having written a song by the same name. But I veered our attention back on track.

"So you must know David pretty well."

"Sometimes a bartender gets to know a guy better than anyone. If he's a good listener."

"Are you a good listener?" I asked, and sipped a little vodka.

"I am," he said proudly, as if he were a soldier and I'd just asked him if he could fight.

"David come in here with his daughter often for dinner?"

"Hardly ever. Matter a fact, I can't recall ever seeing her in here before that night."

"But he brings a lot of other young girls in here, though," I said, letting the remark hang in the air waiting for one of us not to let it fall. I put a little English on it. "It's OK. I know you're discreet. David and I . . . well I'm a detective, right? I check people out. I know a bit about his, shall we say, likes and dislikes. Young girls, for one thing."

The Scot looked slightly relieved, as if I'd excused him from having to make a choice he wasn't having an easy time with.

"Yeah, well, David's not unlike most of the guys who come in here. I mean, you and I both know that young girls are not what they used to be."

He had a point. I'd heard it more eloquently expressed, but I wasn't passing judgment. I just wanted information.

"Has David been in since Tuesday night?"

Stephen looked into an empty glass he was drying as though it were a crystal ball that hid yesterday inside. Most people looked for their answers in full glasses. Not too many answers came from either one.

"Once," he said finally.

"When?"

"I think it was the night after he and the girl, his

daughter, you say, were in."

"Some young cutie?"

"No, as a matter of fact, it was a guy."

"What'd he look like?"

He thought for a second, made a drink with the soda hose while he thought, and finally gave me a description of a guy in his mid-forties, well-dressed, slightly graying hair, medium build, who smoked a pipe.

I paid my tab and thanked the Scot. He'd given me a good drink and some hefty food for thought. The guy he described sounded a lot like Simon Bernstein, the late Edward Smith's lawyer. The man David St. John said he's hadn't seen in years.

Although Penny Silverstein didn't drink, she was a night person, and being so, was always a good person to call when you'd had enough laughs from Dial-A-Prayer. I found a phone booth near the restrooms inside the California Club and gave her a buzz.

"Hello. I hope you're having a wonderful night."

Penny's greeting always made me feel as though I were stuck in a time warp of the sixties, or that maybe she had incurred a head injury while working in a bumper sticker factory.

"Hi. This is Ace," I said, as if I were talking with a normal person.

"Oh, hi," she said, genuinely enthused to hear from me. But then, she seemed genuinely enthused about most things. "You find Kathy yet?"

"No," I said.

"You will, I just know it. She must be somewhere."

I couldn't argue with that. And even if I could, I don't think I would. Not with Penny.

"Hey, Penny, what are you doing right now?"

"Besides talking with you, I was reading about life on Pluto."

"Interesting," I said. It was totally wacko, but it *was* interesting. "You up for some camomile at the Old World?"

"Sure. Give me a half hour, though. I just want to finish the part about the dogs that landed in the Pyrenees during the time of Christ."

"Yeah, that would be a tough place to break away. All right. I'll see you in about thirty minutes."

About an hour and two Stolichnayas later Penny walked in in an Indian print knee-length dress and sandals. Her hair was up and she had on a minimum of makeup. Thirty minutes late was the same as on time for Penny. She had a thing about time. She couldn't tell it. Or maybe she wasn't in it.

"It's really interesting about the dogs," she said, as she sat down and ordered her tea. By the time the waitress returned with Penny's camomile, I'd heard enough bizarre theories about dogs and their significance to our evolution and planetary direction to cause me to take a second look at any canine I saw for the next few months. I'm not entirely over it even now.

"You know, Penny, I'd really like to talk a little about Kathy, if you don't mind."

"No problem. What do you want to know?"

"I met her boyfriend, Bill Jamison."

"Yes?"

"Do you know him well?"

"I met him at Kathy's several months ago. He seems nice enough." But everyone seemed nice enough to Penny. It really meant nothing. At least to me. To Jamison, well, who knows.

"Does he seem on the up and up to you? This is just between you and me. I know you wouldn't want to say anything negative about anyone. But this might be helpful in finding Kathy."

"It would be planting a bad seed to talk bad about

someone else without that person there to present their side of the story."

"So I've heard." Some of my acquaintances hadn't heard, or else didn't care. Some might have even produced bumper crops of negativity from what I know of what they said about me. "All I want is your honest take on the guy. Come on, you can do that."

She sipped at her tea and lingered on the thought for a while. Then she said, "I did tell Kathy that I felt she could find someone more spiritually suited to her than Bill."

That was like saying the Ku Klux Klan could find a better recruit than Huey Newton.

"Anything else?"

"Bill is a very materialistic person."

"Couldn't prove that by the way he lives," I said.

"That may be, but his interests are purely material."

"How so?"

"He and Kathy used to go to her friend's boat in the Marina . . ."

"Josh Wade's boat?"

"Yes. Anyhow, they'd go there usually every weekend. And to hear Bill tell it, he and Josh were as close as midnight and 12:00 A.M."

"They weren't?" I said, sipping on my vodka, picking up a dissonant quality in her voice.

"Oh, they were friendly, but only because of Josh's devotion to Kathy. Frankly, I think Bill may have been taking advantage of Kathy."

That was the closest thing to an indictment you were going to get from Penny. "In what way?"

"Bill Jamison is a hustler. Basically, I see some potential for good in him, but there were things that bothered me."

The old basic-good-in-each-of-us routine. Personally, I thought we were all basically good. Unfortunately, all the best sensations seemed to be bad.

"Anything in particular make you feel that way?"

"For one thing, I know he was playing around on Kathy."

"You see him with another girl?"

"No."

"Then . . .?"

"I went to bed with him once," she said, as though it were an understandable, logical response. "And he told me about others."

"Penny," I said, trying not to sound as surprised as I was. "You went to bed with your friend's boyfriend?"

"Yes. It isn't that hard to understand. After all, it was just sex," she said, as if sex was just another word for taking out the trash.

"I hadn't thought it was anything else. Still, doesn't that make you feel guilty?"

"Absolutely not. There was no involvement whatsoever on either of our parts. We promised never to tell Kathy. And we both had fun."

"You promised not to tell your friend?"

"Technically, it didn't concern her. There are those in our culture who would argue otherwise. But it was simply a biological stimulation and consummation between two people—a commitment of minimum duration. The only way it could possibly affect Bill and Kathy's relationship or my relationship with Kathy was if Bill or I felt guilty about it."

"Or if Kathy found out."

"That, too."

"But I thought you said Bill was too materialistic?"

"He is. I could tell that from making love with him."

"Like reading tea leaves?"

"Much more conclusive than tea leaves."

There was logic in there somewhere. However, I think it was being held captive by an army of lunatics.

"You only slept with him once?" I asked.

"Just once. That was enough. He's not my type. Too small."

"I beg your pardon?"

"He's too small. He's got a very narrow point of view on life. He wants to be a millionaire by the time he's thirty and own a yacht—you know, the whole ugly greed cycle."

"Yeah, well, I was never into it." Maybe I was just never into it as much as I wanted to be. "How does he plan to pull it off?"

"That's another thing. He hasn't got a clue. He just wants the money and what it can buy. He isn't skilled at anything, except maybe using people."

"Which brings us back to Kathy."

"Right."

"What do you know about Josh Wade?"

"Very little firsthand. I went with Kathy and Bill one weekend out to Josh's boat. Bill didn't want me to go. Anyhow, that was the only time I ever went."

"Kathy ever talk about her relationship with Josh? They seem very close."

"I think Josh represents a father image to Kathy. As I'm sure you know by now, Kathy and her real father, David St. John, are not close."

"So I've heard."

"Whenever Kathy had a problem she couldn't solve, she'd turn to Josh. At least since I've known her."

"How did Josh feel about Kathy's relationship with Jamison?"

"He seemed to tolerate it because of Kathy's feelings about Bill."

"What are those feelings? Does she really care about him?"

"She seems to."

"What does she get from the relationship?"

"Tell you the truth, I don't know. What does anyone get from a relationship? To someone looking in from the outside, it might appear to be nothing. She's from a rich family, he's from poor parents and a broken home. He lived with his mother in Venice until just a few years ago. She died. They were on welfare most of the time."

"They have one thing in common. Each one's mother is dead. What about Bill's father?"

"He left Bill and his mother when Bill was three."

"So Kathy and Bill also seem to have reason to dislike their fathers. Say, how do you know so much about Bill?"

"The night we spent together he was pretty talkative. We'd been smoking a little and he got real melancholy. He started reminiscing."

"Does Bill have any friends you know about? Anyone who could tell me more about him?"

"No friends I know about. But he works a few nights a week at a little bar down in Venice. The Coastal Cruiser. You might try there."

"Sounds good. Penny, you've been mighty helpful."

"I hope so."

I bought her another cup of tea and myself another shot of vodka. We talked for another half hour or so about Hollywood, the spiritual implications of Skylab, and the dogs on Pluto.

The next morning I went to see Everett Gray. He lived in Echo Park in an apartment at the top of one of those hills. Jackson Browne and Glen Frey of the Eagles had lived there, as well as several other well-known contemporary celebrities. Before they made it. Echo Park had some charm, which was probably left over from its better days. And the view from the hill I was driving up was kinda nice.

The man who answered the door had a gray moustache and was balding slightly. I introduced myself. He smiled widely and eyed me in a not-too-subtle manner. He was wearing purple briefs, which, he explained, he had been wearing while sunning himself on his porch. He grabbed a robe—he hadn't bothered to grab it until after he had exposed himself to me—offered me a drink, which I refused, and a seat, which I took. He sat down opposite me.

"Life's so funny, you know," he piped up, handing me my line.

"How so?" I said, on cue.

"Well, just last night Elanor—that's my landlady—said that a handsome, brooding stranger would come into my life."

"Yes?" I said as dumbly and unbroodingly as I could.

"Well, I . . . ." He left the "I" lying there waiting for me to dot it. I didn't.

"You sure you wouldn't like some tea, Ace?"

He felt comfortable with my name. Most people didn't. I liked that, but not enough to want to lie in my briefs on his porch and sun myself.

"Mr. Gray," I began.

"Everett. Please, call me Everett."

"Everett, I'd like to ask you a few questions about the St. Johns."

A strange thing happened in his eyes when I said the name. It happened in a place where I couldn't get a good hold on it and it hid too quickly for me to see its color or shape. The only thing I got was a scent. The fragrance was fear. I know. I've worn it a lot myself.

"What do you want to know?"

"I understand you did the obituary on Ellen St. John just after she died."

"I did a lot of writing about Ellen St. John back in those days. After all, I wrote the society page and she *was* Society."

"Did you know her well?"

He played with the ends of his robe belt and looked

away from my eyes. He was looking at something, some-body, somewhere. Wherever it was, it was private and he was deciding whether or not to take me there.

"I knew her quite well," he said finally. "I wrote a great deal about Ellen St. John, but I wrote only about the *social* Ellen St. John. The other side of Ellen, the side that I found the most provocative, was never written about."

"Would you care to explain that?"

"What do you know about Ellen?" He was giving me a tryout. If I passed the test, he'd be ready to play ball.

"Well, first of all, I know that Ellen St. John fooled around a lot on her husband."

He laughed at that, much in the same way someone would laugh if you were to say you were of the opinion that *Playboy* magazine contained sexual material. I began to feel that maybe I had understated myself out of the big leagues.

"Everybody knows *that*," he said, fooling with the hairs of his moustache now. "But that's like saying that a game was played. Without knowing the score, it's meaningless."

"And you know the score?" I said to the sportscaster.

"As a matter of fact, I do," he said coyly. The way he said it sounded like the end of a sentence.

"Care to tell me?"

"Ace, I've been a pillar of discretion all my life—well, almost," he said, chuckling to himself about some cartoon that popped up on his own private video screen. "You see, in my business—the society page biz—discretion is important. Also, in my private life discretion is an important factor." He smiled again real wide. The invitation was there and now it was engraved. He wanted me to know that he was discreet enough so that my reputation wouldn't be soiled. My reputation, what was left of it, needed a little soiling now and then. So that wasn't the reason I passed up Gray's invitation. Just personal preference. Jenny Ling had made a raving hetero out of me.

"What do you think happened to Ellen St. John?" I said finally.

"Just what it said in the papers. I called a few people in Switzerland myself—it was a major happening, let me tell you—just to make sure. She *was* killed in a skiing accident. Poor dear."

"You know the daughter?"

Again that funny look peeked at me through his eyes and retreated again just as quickly.

"Met her a few times when I'd go over to the St. Johns'. Cute little thing. Must be quite a lady by now."

"She is," I said, wishing I could offer a more definitive opinion on the subject.

"What about David St. John?"

"What about him?"

"Did you ever meet him?"

"Many times. I can't say that David and I were ever close. One of those instant dislike numbers, you know."

That I did know.

"You ever meet Josh Wade?"

"Yes. Of course," he said, as if I'd asked him if he brushed his teeth regularly.

"The way I hear it," I said, "he and Ellen were much more than close." I was improvising a little, but I was running out of material.

"Maybe you know more than I gave you credit for. Maybe not. But certainly Ellen and Josh were . . . close."

"But Josh was married at the time, wasn't he?"

"I'm sorry if the subject offends you, Ace, but extramarital sex does happen."

That I knew, too.

"You know, Ace, I've really got to get a few more minutes in the sun. It's fall, and days like this are hard to come by." He looked at me as though he wished I would eject from my seat through the roof and out of his life.

"Yeah, well, thanks for talking with me, Everett. You've been very helpful."

"I doubt that, but thanks for saying so. I hope we meet again someday under more . . . social circumstances."

He showed me out and I could see him watching me as I got into my car.

It was getting to be late in the afternoon, but it was still a beautiful day, so I decided to drive out to the Marina to see Josh again. The weather wasn't the only reason. I didn't need much of an excuse to go to a place where women walked around nearly naked. It was kind of strange, I thought. When I was a kid, if you saw a woman wearing what would now be considered baggy shorts and a confining bra, you were getting an eyeful. And the poor girl being ogled would sometimes scream her embarrassment. Nowadays, down on the beach a G-string smaller than some strippers wear and a couple silver dollars on a string were enough to get you legally on the beach. And those same girls would probably be uptight about being seen in their underwear. Life was crazy all right. But on a planet where human life is supposedly the most cherished quantity and killing is the favorite sport, you're bound to find inconsistencies.

As I approached the slip where Wade's boat was docked, I heard a loud voice coming from the main cabin. The consummately composed Wade was yelling into the phone at someone. Billy was standing outside, maybe trying to give Wade some distance. She saw me as I was about to step aboard. She went quickly below deck and told Wade I was there. The shouting stopped and I heard a noise like a receiver being slammed onto its cradle.

Billy came out first and stood a one-dimensional smile

up for me. She looked as though it took all her strength to do so. Then Wade appeared. He came directly toward me and we shook hands. He didn't bother to put on a false face for me, I'll give him that. He was still moderately upset, but in control.

"Trouble?" I asked, my normal inquisitive, irritating self.

"Oh, hell," he said, curling a corner of his mouth into a snarl of disgust. "Those sons of bitches over at Hamilton Marine promised me I'd have an engine part by yesterday and the damned thing hasn't arrived yet. I'm one of their most loyal customers, and when I'm promised something, I don't expect it just to be a come-on to get me to buy. That kind of thing irritates me, Mr. Carpenter."

"What kind of thing?"

"When a man promises me he will deliver on a particular date and then breaks that promise. I didn't put a gun to his head. He assured me that it would be here at a certain time, I took him at his word, and now I'm screwed."

"It's an important part?"

"Oh, I can go out for short runs, but if I want to take a real trip, I simply cannot. Not until they deliver the part."

I couldn't be too upset about Wade not receiving his yacht part when people in other parts of the world were wondering if they were going to eat again, but I could understand that it was a definite inconvenience.

"So what can I do for you, Mr. Carpenter? Hope you didn't want to go for a long trip."

"No. I just wanted to ask you a couple questions." I was talking to Wade, but I was looking at his wife. She got the message.

"I hope you'll excuse me, Mr. Carpenter, but I have some shopping to do in the Marina."

"Certainly. Nice to see you again," I said.

She grabbed a straw bag with some green and pink flower decorations on the outside and headed off toward the commercial area of the Marina.

"I've been talking to a few people about Kathy St. John and her family. Specifically, the family as it existed about ten years ago."

"Why don't we step inside," said Wade, looking at me as though I might have a disease he didn't want his neighbors to catch. In a way, I guess I did. We walked down into the cabin and I sat down on a semicircular couch that wound partially around a white table. Wade sat down across the table from me.

"Drink?"

"No, thanks," I said. He didn't bother to fix himself one this time. I think I had his full attention.

"I'll get right to the point. I have a feeling that something important in finding Kathy St. John happened ten years ago. I'm trying to find out what that is. I know it doesn't sound logical, and chances are, I'm trying to play ice hockey on a pool table, but I play my hunches."

"How does all this concern me?" he said, as if he had a pretty good idea how it did.

"I've been talking with a few people, and it seems that you and Kathy's mother, Ellen St. John, were very close."

"I told you as much when we talked before."

"You didn't tell me as much as I'm asking now."

"Are you *asking* now?"

"Let's say I'm telling."

"Why should I answer that? Ellen's dead and there's no reason to go into the matter."

"I'm not trying to unfold anyone's dirty laundry. What she did and what you did, or do, are of no concern to me as long as it doesn't relate to finding Kathy St. John. Look, I'm not trying to blackmail you, if that's what you're thinking."

The word blackmail made his eye twitch a little; like

he'd seen it before and it hadn't treated him nice.

"Blackmail is a possibility for a man with my money, Mr. Carpenter." It didn't seem like a big possibility, at least for marital infidelity. After all, we lived in modern times and this was the West Coast. The Marina, for chrissakes. His wife, if she didn't know, might be pissed, maybe not, but I doubt if he would be afraid of losing his marriage. And he wasn't a political figure. Blackmail sounded reasonable, a familiar song, but there was a sour note somewhere that I just couldn't quite make out.

"So did you have an affair with Ellen St. John?"

He looked at me with a pained expression, as though I'd just asked him to remove his front tooth with a pair of tweezers. Then, after a sigh, he resignedly said, "Yes. Are you satisfied?"

I didn't feel like propping up my pillow and having a smoke, but I was glad to get an answer. "OK. I see."

"No, you don't see," said Wade, suddenly taking the offensive. "Ellen was a fine woman and my admission deserves an explanation. Ellen and David were husband and wife only in a legal sense. David's life was defined in terms of legalities, the objective senses of things. He lived life on a most superficial level. Ellen, on the other hand, was a passionate woman who loved life and knew it had to be lived to be enjoyed. She was caught in an untenable position. She didn't want to divorce David, but she wanted to experience more of a life than he was willing to give."

The whole thing was sounding like some pretty cheap rationale, the kind of thing that would only last an episode or two on the soaps and I could hardly believe that a man like Wade was part of the cast. The director maybe, but not someone animated by the bouquet of some second-rate writer's cheap-wine wanderings.

"So you provided her with what she needed at the time."

"An oversimplification, certainly, but basically, yes. We shared a common reality. Our sensitivity to life's pleasures provided a strong bond. But it only lasted a few years."

"Why did it end?"

"I'm married, as you can see. I was married then, and my marriage comes first."

Wade had an interesting sense of priority.

"Did she have other lovers who you know about?"

"Ellen was not promiscuous, not the kind of person you're making her out to be. It sounds so cheap."

"Maybe I should say it differently." But I didn't. "When did all this happen?"

"It was primarily during the early stages of her marriage."

"Primarily?" I said, asking for trouble.

"Look, Mr. Carpenter, I trust you mean well, and I'm as concerned as you are about Kathy's safety—undoubtedly more so, I'd say—and if you could show me any relevance in your line of questioning I'd be more than happy to oblige. But you seem lost to me and I'm not about to needlessly impugn, even remotely, the dignity of a good friend to help you find your way back on track. So, is there any *other* way I can be of help?"

"I don't suppose you've heard from Kathy?" I said.

"Certainly not. And even though David and I are not on the best of terms, I would call him straightaway to set his mind at ease. You can be assured of that."

I was assured of nothing. But I said, "OK."

"Did David St. John ever find out about you and Ellen?"

"I don't know for sure, but I think that it's possible he knows what happened."

I passed Billy Wade on my way back down the walkway and we nodded and smiled cordially at each other. She must have been a number in her day. She was still a pretty round figure even now. Ellen St. John must have been pretty persuasive stuff to distract Wade. But then, sometimes it's not the obvious things about a woman that hook you.

On my way out of the Marina I stopped by Hamilton Marine Supply. There were only two guys working, one behind a desk and the other standing idly by a sleek catamaran on the showroom floor.

"Nice cat," I said.

The man came to life as though somebody had just plugged him in. "She's a honey, isn't she." I wondered why boats were always referred to as women. Maybe because sailors liked the idea of going down below to sleep in something they all called she. It got lonely at sea, I guess. Hell, I didn't know.

"Yeah, she sure is. Sleek," I said. It sounded like the right word. If it weren't, I'm sure the salesman wasn't about to correct my word choice.

"Very," he said, as if I'd said something profound. "You in the market for a cat?"

"Well, I've been thinking about it for a while. I was just in the neighborhood visiting Josh—Josh Wade. You know Josh?"

The salesman got a funny grin on his face as though I'd just ask him who was buried in Grant's Tomb. "Do I know Josh!" It wasn't a question. "Who do you think sold him the *Last Resort?*"

"No kidding. You must be . . ."

"Al Michaels."

"Right. Al. He was telling me this morning that he was a little upset with the service he'd been getting here and well, I don't mind telling you that service is an important factor in a purchase of this nature."

He looked more hurt than insulted. "Why, I don't mean to contradict Mr. Wade, but I'm not aware of any problem he's having. I haven't talked with him for about a week or two, but the last time we did, everything was just fine."

"Then maybe he was talking with some other salesman," I said.

"Not likely. You see, although this is not entirely a commission job, we get bonuses for major sales and Mr. Wade is my customer—besides being a personal, though not close, friend. The other two men who work here know Mr. Wade, and our customer-salesman relationship would be respected, I'm quite sure. And if he were having any problems I know he'd let me know. Yes, yes, I'm afraid you must have misunderstood Mr. Wade.

"Now, about this cat," he said.

"I'm going to have to think on it. Could you give me some literature to take with me?"

"Certainly," he said, and disappeared. He returned with a brochure and his card and I told him I was serious. I wasn't even sincere, but he believed me.

As I drove back into Hollywood I was thinking, but things were about as clear as the L.A. skyline. One thing I was sure of—Wade had lied to me. What I didn't know was *why*.

I decided to drive past Maureen's on the way over to the West L.A. station to see Eddy. I don't know what I expected to see, but I couldn't help but think that Maureen knew more than she was telling. Seemed like everybody did. After all, she was seen arguing with Edward Smith the night before he was shot and their conversation had so upset Smith that night he had cancelled dinner with Bernstein and Kitty Jacobs. I didn't really imagine she'd hidden any clues in the front yard, but it was on the way.

As I drove past, I saw a woman at the door. The woman was dressed in a gray skirt and matching jacket. It was Kitty Jacobs. I went around the block and parked my car. By the time I got back, there was no one standing at the door. I tiptoed gingerly around back to the window through which I'd seen Maureen and her slave go through their paces. By the time I reached my post, I heard loud voices. Kitty was not herself, or at least not the self she had shown me at the Beverly Hills Hotel. I couldn't make out the words, but I could see the two women standing toe to toe in Maureen's living room. Apparently Maureen had not asked Kitty to sit down, and it didn't look as though Kitty was acting nice enough to be asked.

The shouting match halted for an instant and Maureen stood defiantly, hands on hips, smiling a wicked smile in Kitty's direction. Then Kitty made a mistake. She slapped Maureen, the way ladies used to slap John Wayne when he'd just laugh. But Maureen wasn't John Wayne.

Maureen's smile disappeared and she jerked a knee up into a place where "ladies" were not supposed to hit each other, and the conservative Ms. Jacobs doubled up, grabbing herself between her legs, and crumpled to the floor with a shrill cry and a gasp. Maureen grabbed Kitty by the arm and dragged her out of the living room, out of my sight. I went around front and stood behind a shrub until Maureen had shut the door, depositing a moaning Kitty Jacobs on the front step.

I approached Kitty, who was now on her feet, though still doubled over with her hands on her knees.

"Kitty," I said.

She looked up, startled. There were a few tears running down her cheeks, but she tried to pull herself together. "What . . . what are you doing here?"

"I was just in the neighborhood," I said, trying to make her feel comfortable with a light remark. "Look, my car's just around the corner, so why don't you let me buy you a drink? Looks like you could use one."

I convinced her, and as we drove down Sunset Boulevard I explained that I'd seen what had happened at Maureen's. Kitty was pretty much recovered, though understandably not in a good mood by the time we got to Mirabelle's. I ordered Pimm'ses for us both and Spike gave me a funny look. He'd never seen me with a woman like Kitty Jacobs. I'd never been "with" a woman like Kitty Jacobs before, and I wasn't thinking about it just then. Although thoughts like that were never faraway.

"I could see a lot, but I couldn't hear what was going on," I said, as Spike set our drinks in front of us. Kitty was thinking about whether to tell me or not.

"Look, I get along a lot better with Maureen than you do. I could get her version of it," I lied. I was really in no hurry to confront Maureen about anything.

"All right. I thought, and still think, that Maureen was blackmailing Edward. Mr. Carpenter," she said, a little condescendingly, "I'm no babe in the woods. I understand that these kinds of things go on. I've had a private detective do a little digging on Maureen Styles and I know what her business is. Being who he was, Edward knew his private life was always under close scrutiny. And a thing like this, whereas it *shouldn't* make any difference, *could* prove embarrassing."

"How did you find Ms. Styles?"

"I got her name and address from the sign-in sheet for Edward's lecture."

"Do you think she's mixed up in Edward's killing?" I asked, although I'd already reached my own conclusion about that.

"It wouldn't make sense if she were blackmailing him, now would it," she said, as if she were explaining that two and two *didn't* equal five.

"And she would hardly leave her name and address, especially after having such a highly visible fight with him the night before he was killed," I continued.

"Precisely."

"What do you think the fight was about?" I asked.

"I believe she was applying pressure, maybe threatening Edward with exposure. I can't be certain."

"Had you ever seen Mr. Smith act that way before?"

"Quite frankly, no. That's why I hired an investigator. Edward was always such an even-tempered man."

"During your investigation, did your detective run across any information that would tie Edward Smith or Maureen Styles to Kathy St. John?"

"Absolutely none. In my opinion the two are totally unrelated."

"Why would Edward Smith, wounded and dying, call Kathy St. John instead of you or Bernstein, or his wife?"

She raised her eyebrows and tilted her head in a "you-got-me" kind of look. "I can't explain that."

Neither could I, but I felt that if I could, I'd be close to finding Kathy. We finished our drinks and I took her back to her car. Then I drove over to see Eddy. He was sitting behind his desk, in a white shirt and brown pants, chin deep in a pile of papers. He looked up at me as though I were a waterboy and he was lying in the desert.

"Ace! Am I glad to see you. I needed a living, breathing excuse to take five." He got up, grabbed his coat, and we were off.

Eddy and I settled in at Figaro's, just a few blocks from the station, and ordered a couple of imported beers. The clientele there were like characters out of a Horatio Alger novel waiting for a mysterious benefactor to turn their nightmares into dreams-come-true. But benefactors were few and far between and those who existed weren't the magnanimous type.

"Got anything new on the St. John case?" asked Eddy.

"I talked to Everett Gray and I think he knows something."

"Like what?"

"Damned if I know, but talking with him was enough to make me think I'm on to something. You sure he's clean except for that parade violation?"

"It woulda come up on the sheet, Ace. I can't pul
out of a hat."

"You know anything about Josh Wade?"

"Zero. Why?"

"He's an old and disengaged friend of the St. Jo
clan of years ago. But he still stays in close contact wi
Kathy."

"Can't lock him up for being friendly."

"Maybe not this year, but I think they're working
it. Anyhow, he lied to me this afternoon. Don't kno
why. He used to be Ellen St. John's lover."

"So what does that have to do with Kathy's disa
pearance and her involvement with Edward Smith?"

"I honestly don't know, but if it had nothing to
with it, I get the feeling I'd be hearing the truth a litt
more often."

"Maybe. Maybe you've just got a face people have
lie to."

I rattled the cubes in my glass a little and gave Edo
a stare that let him know I wasn't amused. He laughe
it off.

"Any luck running down the guy who shot Smith?"
asked finally.

"Not much. Hey, didn't you say that St. John had a
Oriental working for him?"

"That's right. And he wasn't there the second time
met with St. John. But the guy drives a red Toyota, or s
St. John says. Not even close to the description of th
car given by the dishwasher at the Kazkav."

"I'll get the name of St. John's houseboy and check i
out, just in case."

"Good idea."

"Well, I've got to be getting back to work."

"Isn't this called drinking on the job?"

"Nah. I'm working overtime. Haven't been home
since yesterday. Keeps me going."

"Uh ha."

"So where ya off to tonight?"

"Thought I'd make it down to the Coastal Cruiser. Ever hear of it?"

"The one in Venice?"

"That's the one."

"Yeah. I've heard of it. You're gonna have a good time, Ace."

Eddy had a gift for irony.

The Coastal Cruiser was located on Main Street in Venice—actually nearer Santa Monica than Venice. It had a large, saloon-type bar. A propeller fan hung from the ceiling. A dozen potted palms gave the place an ambience not unlike that of the nightclub in which Bogie told Sam to play it again. But it was all the guys sitting with one another that gave the place a real gay atmosphere.

I smiled politely at a few young men in beards and jeans as I entered and made my way to the bar. I saw Jamison taking an order at a table near the back. At the rear of the Coastal Cruiser were couches and coffee tables, which created a relaxed, almost pubby feel.

I walked to where Jamison was standing and tapped him on the shoulder. He looked very surprised to see me. There.

"I'd like to have a word with you."

"What about?"

"I'd like to talk about Kathy."

"You found her yet?"

"No. If you really wanted her found, I think you'd want to cooperate. I'm beginning to think you don't want me to find her."

"Why wouldn't I want you to find her?"

"You got me wondering."

"All right, all right. Step out back into the alley. Through that door," he said, tilting his head in the direction of a door at the rear of the bar. "I'll take care of this order, then I'll take my break and meet you outside."

I said OK and went outside. It was dark and chilly. The ocean was only two blocks away, and through an open space between the bar and the building next to it I could see the moon glistening off the water. It was the perfect setting for romance. Or violence. I wasn't looking for either at that moment.

The back door opened and Jamison stepped outside. He shut the door and walked over to me.

"So what do you want now? The last time we talked you invited the police in for tea and intimidation. Is it just you and me tonight?"

"Just you and me. I was kind of surprised to see you working in a place like this."

"People work in banks. Don't mean they got money."

"Yeah."

"You said you had some things you wanted to ask me. You gonna make me guess?"

That probably would have been a more productive approach, but I didn't think he'd go for it. "I was curious about a few things. How did you meet Kathy?"

Jamison took out a pack of cigarettes, removed one, lit it, put the pack back in his pocket, and blew smoke between me and the ocean. "I met her in a supermarket."

"Which one?"

"You're crazy, you know that. What kind of a detective are you, anyhow?"

I couldn't think of a brand I liked right off, so I just ignored the question. "Humor me, OK?"

"If I'd humor you as much as you want me to I'd be a stand-up comic."

I couldn't picture any routine Jamison would do that'd keep me laughing. "What supermarket?"

"In Hollywood. Ralph's, I think. On Sunset. Now, is that revelatory material?"

"Long way to go for groceries."

"You ever stop and pick something up at the store on your way home?"

"Rarely a lover."

"I was looking for something to eat."

I let that one pass. "So you two just fell in love over the cold cuts and the rest is history."

"You're a wise-ass, Carpenter. The cops got nothin' on me, except not reporting when my girlfriend visited me. And that ain't no crime. And now I'm wastin' my break here in the alley listening to you try to be clever."

"You don't think I'm clever?"

"Look, Carpenter, I'm here because you said I might be able to help you find my old lady. If you've got questions—*real* questions—let's have 'em. If not, shove off."

"How would you characterize your relationship with Josh Wade?"

"All right, I guess. He's real tight with Kathy and we go to his boat a lot. Josh and I get on pretty good. We ain't pals or nothin' like that, but he's all right. No friction."

"Why is Kathy so close to an old family friend who's not on speaking terms with her father?"

"Got me. All I know is Kathy and her old man have never been real loving. Josh's always been interested in Kathy and Kathy likes attention. With Kathy's mother dead and her father shuttling her everywhere but home, I think Josh felt sorry for Kathy. That's what *I* think."

"Kathy ever talk about the days when her mother was alive?"

"Not too often."

"When she does, how does she seem to feel about her mother?"

"Kinda vague. Sometimes she seems bitter, like her

mother deserted her or something. Now that doesn't make any sense at all," said Jamison, puffing on his cigarette. "After all, she died, right?"

"That's what I hear."

"Then sometimes she sounds as though she sympathizes with her mother for having had to live with David St. John. Mostly she just feels cheated at not having a mother around when she was growing up. Or much of a father."

"Would you say she loved her mother?"

"Hard to say. A kid wants to love his parents just because they're his parents. But David St. John is hard to love. And Mrs. St. John wasn't there. I think Kathy sometimes likes to think she loved her mother very much. Everybody needs somebody to love," said Jamison, half-singing the words.

"Kathy ever talk about her mother's relationship with Josh Wade?"

"Relationship? What do you mean?"

"Just a relationship. You and I have a relationship, though on the scale of one to ten it's hardly on the board."

"She remembers Josh being closer to her mother than to her father. And that sometimes Josh and her mother would take her places, like the zoo and the circus. Kids' stuff, you know."

"Did Kathy ever mention the name Edward Smith to you?"

"Never. Hey, look, my break's about up."

"Fine. You've been very cooperative."

"Don't count on it again. Come more prepared if there *is* a next time." With that, he turned his back to me and went inside.

I decided not to return through the Coastal Cruiser, so I walked through a thin alleyway to the front walk. Just as I was about to get into my car, I saw a familiar face entering the bar. It was the face of Everett Gray.

* * *

I went to a phone booth across the street from the
Coastal Cruiser and called my answering service. St.
John had called. He wanted me to come over to his place
on the double. I called first, but he said he didn't want
to talk on the phone. He sounded unnerved. I'd never
heard or seen him that way before. Something had happened.

It was about 10:00 P.M. by the time I got to Blue Jay
Way and St. John's top-of-the-hill roost. I rang the bell
and he let me in. I thought about asking if it was still the
Oriental's day off, but decided to wait. He didn't offer
me anything to drink. He must've been upset.

"I have received a ransom note, Mr. Carpenter."

"Got it handy?" I replied, as though he'd just told me
he'd received a brochure from Sears.

He reached in his smoking jacket pocket and handed
me an envelope. Whatever fingerprints might have been
on the paper were probably obscured now by St. John's.
And besides, most criminals watched enough television
to know to wear gloves when handling a kidnap note.
The envelope was unstamped. It had been hand-de-
livered and had been in St. John's mailbox when he'd
picked up his mail earlier in the day, or so he said.

It was a standard note. We've got Kathy. Twenty-five
thousand dollars gets her back unharmed. Instructions
will follow tomorrow A.M. by phone. Involve police and
we'll send your daughter back in pieces. So far, it was
strictly *Charlie's Angels* shtick.

"Doesn't twenty-five thousand seem like a pretty
small sum?" I asked. Twenty-five thousand dollars was
a hunk of money to me, and about as real to me as bicy-
cling to Greenland.

"It is a small sum. And I certainly intend to pay it. It
sounds like a prank perpetrated by one of the low-life
types my daughter hangs around with. Not *really* a criminal. A bum, a no-good, perhaps, but not a professional

criminal. The money will just go for drugs and good times. After I get my daughter back, such an incompetent should be easy to locate. When I do, he will wish he'd never dreamed up kidnapping my daughter."

"I take it you're not talking about having him arrested."

"Arrest and short-term imprisonment often don't leave much of a lasting impression on the wrongdoer."

"And you've got a better idea."

"The less said about that, the better."

"So what do you want me for?"

"I'd like you to deliver the money." I *had* noticed that the kidnappers hadn't specified that he'd have to drop it off himself. I was afraid that's where I came in. St. John anticipated my next question.

"Of course, even though you are currently in my employ, I will pay you extra for performing this task. How does an extra thousand dollars sound?"

It sounded like my favorite song. But usually I could hear it for a cheaper price.

"OK," I said. "The note says to wait for a call tomorrow morning."

"That's right. Go home and get some sleep and come back about 9:00 A.M. If they call before then, I'll call you at your home number."

"I'd like to ask you a few questions," I said, after it became obvious I wasn't quite ready to leave.

"Yes?"

"First, I see that your Oriental houseboy is not here again today. Still his day off, or is he on vacation?"

"I'm afraid I had to let Michael go."

"Were you holding him?" I asked, making him spell out what was probably a spur-of-the-moment story.

"I fired him, Mr. Carpenter. I'm sure you knew what I meant."

"Do you know where I can reach him?"

"I don't. I'm sorry."

Blenders is Club Topic

September meeting for the Fairview Extension Homemakers Club was held at the home of Olive Netz September 9, at 1:30 p.m. The program theme for that day was "Blender Adventure" presented by Imelda Garcia, extension home economist.

Extension Homemaker Club meetings are held monthly at individual homes and public sites and interested persons should contact the County Extension Office for further information on the Extension Homemakers Club program.

ENDS TRAINING

Army Pvt. Joe W. Salazar, son of Cora Salazar of Fairview, ha completed a 12-w training period combat training advanced training at Ga.

c... and
because
tion and
is parcel
cult and
or the
ge (Sec.
Land
agement
ce with
2(b), a
petitive
ng land
go, has
o be in
st for
s:
rain
ract
s a
ent
tr.
as
ol
of
d

woman ...
there to say?

A new Headstar...
parent policy council, to
be formed sometime this
month, must approve the
staff, according to
federal regulations.

In the meantime, two
of the top administrative
positions have been filled
by people on an acting
basis. Mary Agnes
Martinez is acting
director, and Elias
Archuleta is educational-
social services coor-
dinator.

Superintendent Vigil
has said the program
has been admitting too
many students who did
not qualify by income for
the program, resulting in
the reduction in force.

He had no ready ex-
planation Friday for the
other ten people, who
were not re-appointed
and whose jobs were
filled by others.

BIG ...
Monday-S...

"Me too. What's his name?"

"Michael Yamaguchi."

"You seem like the kind of guy who'd have someone checked out before you'd let them work in your home."

He stretched his neck a little uneasily as if his collar were getting tighter. "I think I have his home address and social security number written down somewhere."

"And his phone number?" I prodded.

"Possibly." St. John got up and went into the other room. After a minute or two he came out and, sitting down again, handed me a piece of paper with a name, phone number, and address on it.

"Thanks," I said, and pocketed the paper. "I have two other people I want to ask you about. First, Simon Bernstein."

I watched what the name did to his face. The two collided in an unfriendly way.

"You told me you hadn't seen Simon Bernstein in a long time. Maybe ten years. Is that right?"

He was walking on thin ice and he could feel the water bursting through. "I'm not a liar, Mr. Carpenter." That wasn't an answer.

"A friend of mine told me he saw you and Simon Bernstein at the California Club the night your daughter was shot."

"I did have dinner there with an associate of mine that night, but I assure you that it wasn't Simon Bernstein. There *is* a way to put your mind at ease."

"I can think of a couple."

"You can ask Simon Bernstein himself."

"Or I can ask the man you had dinner with."

"You could, except that man is in Europe now."

"May I have his name?"

"Timothy Watts. He's an art dealer in Beverly Hills."

I had to hand it to St. John. He was quick. Or else he was telling the truth. My guess was that he was quick. I had no doubt that Mr. Timothy Watts was in Europe—

unreachable by me, but probably not by St. John—and, by the time he returned to L.A., would be more than willing to corroborate St. John's story. And I also knew that Bernstein and St. John had probably guaranteed each other that neither would deviate from the story that they had not met. Dead end.

"You ever hear of Everett Gray?" I asked.

"Everett Gray." St. John said the name a couple of times, squinting his eyes as he did so as if trying to see into the past through some bright light. "Name sounds familiar. Definitely not a close friend, past or present."

"He's a newspaper reporter. Society page."

"Ah, yes," said St. John, as if remembering an unpaid bill. "He was a pest. Always making my wife into the goddess of the jet set, which she always wanted to be. A pamperer, a leech. Couldn't even write worth a damn, if I remember correctly."

"When's the last time you saw him?"

"That I can tell you exactly. After I learned of Ellen's accident, I arranged a funeral ceremony just for the immediate family. And this clown showed up. He crashed the funeral service! I've heard of crashing a party, but what kind of human being would crash a funeral! I told him then that I would make him sorry he did that."

"And did you?"

"He was fired from the *Times* shortly after that. I heard he got another job on another paper, but certainly not as prestigious a one as the *Times*."

"That was the last time you saw Everett Gray?"

"That's right."

"OK, that's about it. I think I'll go get some sleep and meet you here tomorrow morning about nine."

"Fine."

As St. John closed the door behind me, I could tell that he was worried. Me? I was starting to worry, too.

       *   *   *

When I got to the bottom of the hill I pulled into a Shell station and used the pay phone. I dialed the number St. John had given me for Michael Yamaguchi. The line was busy. I wasn't real surprised. The address, 1220 North West Knoll, wasn't more than a mile away, so I drove to it.

The neighborhood was pretty nice, mostly one-story houses. There was a huge modern apartment building that spanned an entire block. An orange banner advertised tennis on the roof. Yamaguchi's house was opposite the high-rise courts and looked to be a duplex. Sure enough, there was a red Toyota parked in the driveway. St. John had told the truth about the car, at least.

As I got out of my car, I saw Yamaguchi coming out of his door with an overnight bag in his hand. I walked quickly over to his car and met him at the driver's side just as he was closing the car door.

"Hi," I said.

His head jerked to the place my voice was coming from. He looked me in the eyes and tried to look as though someone stopping him from getting into his car happened all the time.

"Mr. Carpenter. Good evening."

"Going somewhere?"

"Going to stay with my girlfriend," he said.

"Uh huh. I think we ought to go back inside first. There's someone I'd like you to talk with."

"Talk with who?"

"A friend. No big deal," I said, and smiled.

It took Eddy only five minutes to get over to West Knoll from the station. Yamaguchi looked mighty scared when Eddy and a couple of uniformed guys showed up. But that didn't mean much. Such a situation could make an innocent man frightened as hell. I'd seen it happen.

"So where were you last Wednesday in the early afternoon?"

"Every Wednesday I go to class."

"Class?" said Eddy, as though academia was foreign to him. Perhaps it was.

"I take accounting class on Wednesdays from noon to three at West Los Angeles Business College."

"Where is that located?"

"On Beberly."

"Beberly?" said Eddy.

"Beverly," I said.

"Oh, yeah." Eddy was a trip.

"Any way we can verify you were there last Wednesday?"

"Teacher see me. Other students see me. They tell you."

"They better," said Eddy, trying to get tough.

"I hear you aren't working for Mr. St. John anymore," I said.

"He fire me."

"Why?"

"Not know why."

"Didn't he give you any reasons?"

"He say I lazy. I not lazy, but I not argue with him. I get another job. Almost done with accounting school. Get good job soon."

He seemed to be taking his sacking in stride.

Eddy continued to grill him a little more, but came up with nothing even close to booking evidence. Eddy closed the questioning with a promise to check out the accounting school and a warning to Yamaguchi to stay available for more questioning.

I used Yamaguchi's phone to call Jenny. I got lucky. She had the night off and was curled up reading. Jenny was just what I needed. She asked me to come over. She had a nice place on Havenhurst, just off Santa Monica.

It was the upper half of a California stucco, with a balcony and hardwood floors. She'd done a great job fixing up the place and bringing its inherent character to the surface. There was an Oriental screen with hand-painted characters on it that broke the living room into two warm pockets, each with its own charm. The furniture was mostly white and black, and real wood tables finished the aesthetic sentences wherever appropriate. It was about 1:00 A.M. when I knocked on her door.

"Come in," she said, and ushered me into her world with a soft kiss. She led me to her couch and sat me down in front of the coffee table and a waiting Stolichnaya. The lady aimed to please. And she was a sharpshooter. She curled her legs up under her and settled in next to me, waiting for me to speak whenever I felt ready. Even though Jenny had lived in the Western whirlpool, or cesspool, of L.A. for about eight years, she still retained several admirable Eastern, feminine qualities acquired while growing up in Singapore. A willingness—even more than the actuality—of a woman to be submissive to her man I found most seductive. And contrary to popular opinion, I didn't know a man who was not totally charmed by it. But that's easily understood. Where in Western society was it chic to be a submissive woman? The word had a kind of slavish connotation to it that belied the power of its true nature.

"How ya been?" I asked, breaking the ice.

"OK. I just go to dance class and dance at the club at night. Then I come home alone and read. Then I get up the next morning and do it again."

I knew she usually came home alone. She, like most of the girls who worked in the sex business, had personal policies about dating men they met at work. Never do it.

I had met Jenny at a 1940s Detective Film Festival at a theater in the Valley. There, amid the nostalgia and the common bond of being mystery buffs, Jenny and I had become positively enraptured with each other. I hadn't found out for about two months about the club she danced in. All she'd told me in the beginning was that she was studying dance and had a part-time job. That sounded typical. That could have been said by thousands of girls—and guys—in Hollywood. The fact that I was a detective had caused her interest level to overflow, and we took in at least two mystery movies a week—Hollywood is full of theaters that show old movies and occasionally put on mystery festivals.

We'd had the same late-night hours and would often meet late for drinks or a snack and sometimes a late show at her apartment or mine. Though she hadn't said, I'd figured her part-time job was something like an all-night answering service or a cocktail waitress. It might seem funny that I never asked, me being a detective and all, but we were friends first, then lovers. I let her tell me what she wanted to tell me, when she wanted to tell me. I figured she wasn't that proud of her job and with my job being so perfect to our common reality, she just didn't want to break the spell. "You're a detective and I'm a waitress," just didn't sound too magical.

Then one night we were supposed to get together at my place to see *Double Indemnity*. About 1 A.M. she called me. "Ace, I don't think I'm going to be able to make the movie. A girl went home early and I've got to fill in for her." There was silence at her end of the phone. I knew there was something else she wanted to say. Everything up to that point had been good times, and now a funny feeling in my stomach—that feeling you get when you know you're about to get your emotions kicked—started to go through its paces. I swallowed, set down the *TV Guide,* and waited.

"You can come over here, though, if you want."

"Where's 'here'?" I asked.

"The Kit Kat Club on Santa Monica." She had decided to come to grips with the situation. I still don't know whether or not a girl really had had to go home early, or if that was the night she just finally decided to get it all out in the open.

"All right," I said. I knew the place. Everybody did. It was known as the best strip joint in Hollywood. "I'll be over in about a half hour."

She said, "OK," and hung up.

I felt a strange mix of emotions inside. She wasn't having sex with another man, but the same batch of feelings came pouring out. Maybe they weren't the same, but they were in the same family. It was almost as though she were having sex with every man who came into the place. It was a peculiar point of view. Whenever I'd gone to a strip club, I'd viewed the stripper as some sexual object up there who catered to my fantasies, who was screwed and made love to by all of us guys sitting at our tables getting drunk. Kind of like a mental gang bang. The girl was just some slut, we all knew that. So, what the hell.

But now that girl was *my* girl. I was turned around. And a little scared to walk into the place and see *my* girl being mentally felt up by a bunch of drunks. But that was certainly what I was in for, if I went.

At the time, I was feeling a great deal for Jenny. We were both entering an emotional area that was getting awfully close to love. I guess she felt that it was time to be totally honest. I was doing all right financially, but it was obvious I couldn't take her in, pay all her bills, and support her dance habit, too. And she wasn't ready to give up her dance. She'd do it at any cost. She knew the price. She knew it very well, and was about to ask me if the price was too steep for me.

When I walked in Jenny was on stage. She'd just started. She was dancing in a black slit-up-the-side dress and high heels. There were about a dozen guys sitting around. There was a little string around the stage where guys would hang dollar bills. The idea was that when someone laid a dollar bill over the string, the dancer would come over to that spot—where the guy was sitting —and do a little extra bump and grind just for the tipper. I knew the story.

The dress came off to moderate applause. During the second song her bra came off and a few dollar bills began to appear on the string. By this time Jenny was wearing only the tiniest of G-strings. A fat, bald guy wearing a shirt that didn't fit him too well, took out his wallet and hung five one-dollar bills over the string. Jenny danced over in his direction and squatted down in front of him. Then she fell backward and caught herself with her hands, supporting herself so that she was on her back about two feet off the floor, legs spread facing the big spender. He was smiling broadly. All the time she didn't look at me. I knew she'd seen me come in, but she wasn't looking in my direction. She kept doing the blatantly humping motion to the drunken adulation of the crowd. The bald guy reached in his wallet and withdrew a ten-dollar bill and hung in over the string. Then he pointed and made it clear what he wanted for the money. He wanted her to move the crotch of her G-string aside so he could see her femininity. She obliged. He smiled. I felt a little sick. She wasn't holding anything back. For the bald guy, or for me. I got up and went outside for a little air. Luckily that was Jenny's last dance for the night. I waited for her outside. Some tough guy walked her to her car and when I appeared, he looked as though he was hungry and I was food. When Jenny saw me, she called him off.

We took her car and went to a twenty-four-hour coffee shop on Sunset to talk. The words came slowly. Not at all for a little while.

"I've never had sex with any man I've met in there," she said.

It made me feel a little better. But not much.

"I can't quit, honey," she said. "Unless you've got more money than I think you do." She had never called me honey before. I remember that was the first time. "I wanted you to know."

"Now I know. What now?"

"I guess that's up to you. I feel a lot for you, Ace. I haven't felt this way about anyone in my life. But this is not Camelot and I'm no princess. This is Hollywood, and I'm trying to make it in a business everybody says I don't have a chance to be successful in."

I wanted her to convince me. I wanted her to dispel the lessons, the pain, the sense of right and wrong that impinged on me so hard that I felt like I was going to burst into tears.

"I love you, Ace," she said simply. It was the first time she'd said that, too. And it was the best time for her to say it. I could tell she meant it.

Some of the pain began to fall back to the second row. It was still there if I got weak, but I loved Jenny and wanted to see something good in all this. I needed some salve to sooth the wound. It might leave a scar, it might not. At that moment I was just interested in stopping the bleeding.

We missed *Double Indemnity* that night. That was two years ago and we've been close ever since. I've dated other people, she has, too. We cared most for each other, but there was no exclusivity. Every once in a while one of us started to get serious, but it went away. We were comfortable with each other now, and maybe a little in love.

"You look upset," she said. "Something with the St. John case?"

"Yeah," I said, sipping my vodka. "Looks like I'm

going to play real cops and robbers tomorrow."

"Dangerous?"

"I'm dropping off some ransom money for St. John."

"The stuff movies are made of."

"Yeah." I curled the left half of my mouth into a cynical smile.

Then I proceeded to tell her about my conversation with St. John.

"You think he's right about the kidnapper being an amateur?"

"Yes, I do. In fact, if I can swing it, I'm going to drop the money, appear to leave, circle back around to the drop area, and see who picks it up. I won't try to nail the guy and take a chance with Kathy's life—although I don't think an amateur is likely to get involved with murder."

"Sounds exciting," she said, as convincingly as she could. She was into fictional mysteries, celluloid danger, but when it came to my taking real chances, the lady got worried. We'd talked about the risks of my job a long time ago, and the subject had never been brought up again. But the concern, the worry was there in her voice. I could tell. And she could tell I could tell.

She put her drink down and put her head on my lap much the same way a kitten would. I stroked her jet-black, shoulder-length hair and we both were silent for about fifteen minutes. I reached down and picked up the *TV Guide*. There was a Nick and Nora movie on at two. I mentioned it, but Jenny just made a sound. She started to rub the inside of my right thigh and occasionally hugged my leg tightly.

She stood up slowly, liquidly, and tossed her hair back over her shoulders. She extended her hand to me. I put the *TV Guide* down and stood to meet her. She led me into her bedroom. She had a brass bed. A half dozen pillows were strewn all over it. She threw off all but two, pulled down the covers, and told me to sit down. She undressed me, taking off my shoes, socks, outer and under clothes and laid each neatly on a chair at the foot of the bed. Then she took off her robe and gently, sensuously slipped out of her bikini panties. It was nothing like the show at the club. Her body was presented to me on such a different flow, a different wavelength—an aesthetic wavelength—that the two seemed to have about as much in common as Arabs and Jews. Jenny was beautiful. She showed skin to others, she showed herself, her beauty, to me.

She drained the uptightness, anxiety, and fear from my body that night in a way I'll never forget. Every movement, every sensation, every kiss, every thrust carried with it the certainty of deep feeling and love. Yes, I loved Jenny, and at moments like that I could even admit it.

After we made love I called my answering service and told them that if St. John called I'd be at Jenny's number. I told them I'd be there till about six. Then I'd go home, clean up, change, and have some breakfast before going to St. John's.

Jenny and I slept about as close as two people could sleep that night. And we made love a couple more times before I left. When I awoke at six, she was sleeping like an angel. People look so innocent when they're asleep. I got out of bed as silently as I could. She sleepily kissed me through half-awake eyes and fell back to sleep while I dressed. I kissed her lightly on the mouth. I'm not sure whether or not she was awake, but I'm sure I saw her smile when I whispered, "I love you."

I arrived at St. John's about 8:45 after showering, shaving, and eating breakfast at my place. He looked a little nervous when he let me in, which was understandable. A pitcher of juice and two glasses were sitting on the table to which he led me. A phone sat between us also.

"I take it no one has called yet," I said, pouring myself a glass of orange juice.

"No. And the waiting is the difficult part."

"Yeah, the waiting is tough. Had any thoughts on who might try a stunt like this?"

"Just what I said yesterday—one of Kathy's low-life friends."

"Anyone who might have a personal grudge against you?"

As I asked the question a few things came to mind. David St. John was never going to win any popularity contests. His own daughter wasn't too thrilled about him. There was always the chance she was faking the kidnapping. But I knew Smith's death wasn't a trick, and that gave everything else surrounding Kathy's disappearance a sense of seriousness and danger. No one I'd talked to since I started the investigation seemed to give a damn about St. John. And then there was the new ingredient of his firing his houseboy—although Yamaguchi didn't seem like the criminal type. But I'd been wrong pretty regularly in my life. And I didn't feel like I was on a roll.

"There are a few. But this is not the way they would go about getting back at me. Besides, anyone competent enough to *be* an enemy of mine would scoff at the idea of a twenty-five-thousand-dollar ransom. I often make that in a single week. And, though it's none of your business, my holdings run substantially into the millions. My *car* cost more than twenty-five thousand, for God's sake. No, no, it is not an enemy of mine. Look to the scum my daughter hangs out with and there you will find the person responsible for this."

It was interesting that in his entire explanation of the value of the threat against him he talked only of the money involved and not once did he mention that Kathy might be something he considered valuable. But I didn't dwell on it. I was used to his attitude by now.

We sat and made small talk for about a half hour before the call came. I got my ear close enough to the receiver so that both St. John and I could hear what was said.

"Is this David St. John?" the man's voice on the other end of the phone said.

"Yes," said St. John, as though he was accepting a collect call.

"I'm going to make this short and sweet, so listen and get it right the first time."

St. John looked at me with a frustrated anger etching his face hard. He didn't like being talked to that way. He was maniacally proud. I had the feeling he was getting ready to hang up on the guy for being rude. I squinted my eyes and shook my head as if to say it was all right, he'd get his chance.

"I'm sending someone else with the money," St. John said.

"He'd better come alone. I'll be watching. And he'd better not be a cop. If I don't come back with the money, on time, call my partner and give him the password, Kathy's dead. You got that?"

"Yes," said St. John. He seemed to take the threat better than simple rudeness.

"You got the money?"

"I do."

"That's very good, Davy," said the caller, as if to a child who'd just asked for praise for his first crayon drawing. Whoever it was knew how to irritate St. John. The phone was nearly melting in his hand. I was almost beginning to hope the guy got away with the dough and was never heard from again. What St. John would do, or have done, to the guy would be too brutal for me even to hear about.

"Take the money, in a plain brown paper bag, to MacArthur Park. There's a stone wall on the Sixth Street side at the corner of Park Avenue and Sixth.

There are three benches there. There are trash cans next to the far left and far right benches. Put the money in the can closest to the Park Avenue corner at exactly 10:00 A.M. That's one half hour from now. You're only fifteen to twenty minutes away. Leave as soon as I hang up. I'll be watching, and if I see anything funny going on, Kathy's dead," he repeated. "Don't try to be cute. After I get the money, I'll make a phone call. I'm going to drive a while first just to make sure I'm not being followed. I'll be looking for helicopters, too, so don't be stupid. When I'm satisfied no one's following me, I'll make a phone call and say one word into the phone. If it's the right word, Kathy's on her way home. If it's the wrong word, my buddy pulls the trigger. Davy, you ever see someone's brains blown all over the room?"

"Not yet," said St. John. The guy on the other end missed St. John's meaning. I didn't.

"Ten o'clock," said the caller, and hung up.

St. John put down the phone and looked at me.

"Any voice you recognize?" I asked.

"No. But it sounded strange to me."

"He had a handkerchief or something like that over the mouthpiece. Still, it seemed vaguely familiar to me. Certain intonations. However, we don't have time to sit and chat. I've got a half hour."

"I will get you the money. You can find some paper bags in the kitchen under the sink."

I went and got the bags and St. John returned shortly with the money. I had the distinct feeling St. John hadn't had to go to the bank for his money. That could mean a few things, all unimportant to the matter at hand.

"I'll come back here after I make the drop," I told him.

"I will give you your bonus when you return. Now, get going."

With that he showed me out and I was off, headed down a Hollywood hill with twenty-five thousand bucks in cash sitting on the seat next to me.

On the way over I thought about what the caller had said. From the sound of it, it looked like a two-man operation. One guy to pick up the money, one to watch the hostage. I had a couple of ideas about getting cute, but decided against all but one. It might not help me find Kathy, but it would definitely help to get the money back and bring the culprits to justice. Which I thought would be far preferable to having St. John disembowel them.

MacArthur Park must have been something special in its day. But that must have been a distant yesterday. Two Mexican movie houses could be seen from the park, which was still struggling to maintain a certain dignity. Within its boundaries were an amphitheater, a lake, lots of benches, and rolling hills. Chubby, brown-skinned hookers with a week's makeup on their faces and dresses slit up to their chunky thighs patrolled the park in search of cheap tricks. Winos with paper bags full of ninety-nine-cent painkillers sat staring from their benches onto a world that recoiled from them in disgust. Yeah, it was fun, this place.

I parked my car on Sixth, across the street from the drop point. I looked around, but saw no one paying much attention to me. With the bag full of money under my arm, I walked across to the trash can near the Park Avenue corner, I looked around, checked my watch, which now read 9:57, and sat down. I'm the punctual type. I thought 10:00 A.M. on the dot would be a nice touch. I waited two and a half minutes and, after being offered "the best piece on Alvarado for cheap," dropped the bag into the trash can, walked across the street to my car, got in, and drove leisurely away. I even made a lei-surely right turn on Coronado two blocks away. But by the time I hit the next right I was gunning my engine for all it was worth. Two blocks later I was directly behind an office building that fronted the drop sight. I parked my car illegally and raced down a driveway to where an old woman was sweeping her porch. She looked at me as though people regularly ran down her driveway. No big deal. There was a tall fence at the back of the house. I grabbed her garbage can and put it up against the fence. I stood on the garbage can, but the lid was rusted so much that my weight disintegrated it and I fell right through into a bag of gooey trash. I felt like one of those inflatable dolls you push over and they bounce back up. However, being the ingenious detective I am, I extricated myself from my humiliating circumstances and found a piece of wood to place over the garbage can lid. Standing on the wood I was able to lift myself over the fence and, with a fall of about three feet, land safely on the other side. There was a back door to the office building—I used it and raced up a flight of stairs to the front of the building. A window in the hallway looked out on the park. I knelt at the window, trying to keep my face out of sight and still be able to see the trash can that I'd dropped the ransom in. My watch read 10:02. Maybe I'd missed whoever it was who was supposed to pick up the cash, but I'd give it another few minutes.

It got to be 10:15 and still no action. I was getting ready to leave when a guy wearing sunglasses, jeans, a black shirt, and white tennis shoes approached the trash can. I knew who it was. I'd just talked with him recently. It was . . .

My excitement over being so clever was interrupted by a heavy blow on the back of my head that put my lights out for a while.

When I came to I was looking up at a cop. He wasn't sure what to make of me. I didn't smell of alcohol, but I was lying in the right position. I told him I'd been mugged. He asked me what I was doing in the building in the first place and I said I'd stopped to see . . . Dr. Higgins—that was the name on the door below which I was lying. My money was still intact, so the mugging story seemed a little thin. I told him my assailant must have heard someone coming and split. The cop didn't buy that, but he couldn't arrest me for getting hit over the head, so he let me go. As I was being questioned, a woman occasionally peeked out of Dr. Higgins' office. It was probably she who called the cops. After the cop left, I went inside to talk with the woman.

She looked up at me as though I were something evil. I asked her if she had seen anything, but she had only seen me lying on the floor in the hallway. She had come onto the scene after I'd been K.O.'d. She also said she had seen no one coming or going on her way into the office.

I called St. John from Higgins' office and told him I'd be by in about twenty minutes.

By the time I arrived St. John was nervously pacing the floor. He let me in and was wearing a tough look on his face.

"Well, you screwed it up, didn't you?"

I was in no mood to be scolded, but I *had* overstepped my instructions a bit and I knew it.

"The caller said you improvised on the instructions and now *I'm* going to have to pay the price."

"Pay the price? What does that mean?"

"I don't know. That was all he said. And don't expect a bonus for this type of sloppy work."

"Yeah," I said, massaging the lump on my head.

"The caller said he would call back 'later' with more instructions. Now I've got to do it myself."

"Do what?"

"I told you that I don't know. But whatever it is, I'm to be the one to do it."

I just basically wanted to report in, show St. John the

lump on my head, and chat about what an inept detective I was. After that was over I left and drove over to the West L.A. station.

Eddy was filling out papers, eating a ham on rye, and washing it down with lukewarm coffee.

"Eddy, I want to tell you something on the QT. This is not to become official police business. Not yet, anyhow—OK?"

"Is it about the St. John case?"

"Yeah."

"Look, I can't promise anything. It might not be ethical."

"Just for a day or two. Then you got it. I just need to talk to somebody about it."

He pondered my offer for a few minutes and chewed on his sandwich.

"OK, but I reserve the right to use my better judgment."

"Great," I said. I was home free. Eddy hadn't used his better judgment in years, and I guessed he'd probably forgot where he put it.

I told him about the kidnap and ransom number.

"And you saw who made the pickup?" asked Eddy incredulously.

"Yeah. It was Bill Jamison."

"What the hell do you make of that? A guy holds his own girlfriend for ransom to her own father. Some world, eh?"

"Maybe he wanted a dowry."

"Doesn't that seem strange to you, Ace?"

"I read and see and hear things every day that seem stranger than that to me. But, tell you the truth, it just doesn't wash. I have the feeling that something else is going on."

"Like maybe Kathy's in on the whole thing?" Eddy asked, sipping at his coffee.

"Maybe. But I keep going back to Smith's murder.

That's the thing that totally screws up all the theories. I have the feeling that if we knew more about Smith's killing, we'd know more about this whole damn mess."

"Maybe the two are totally unrelated."

"Could be. Could be a million things."

"So why come to me?"

"I'm going to pay Jamison a visit. I didn't tell St. John because he'd have sent in the Marines. I think I can talk with Jamison. We're not close, but I know the language he speaks. I wanted you to know who picked up the money in case something happens to me. I'll call you tomorrow afternoon, if not before. If I haven't called by then, contact St. John, tell him what I've told you. But I think *you* should be in control of things, not St. John."

"I see your point. You're taking a risk."

"Getting up in the morning and walking outside to pick up the paper is a risk nowadays. I just put some excitement into my risks, that's all."

"Any idea who might have given you the goose egg?"

"Not one. Well, actually that's not true. But that's a real shot in the dark, not worth mentioning. I'm sure that if I confront Jamison with what I know, I'm going to get some answers. If the whole matter is still unofficial, I think I can make a few deals that might bring this whole drama to a climax. The fewer bodies the better."

"I got ya."

He did, too. Eddy was a good friend.

The next morning hit me between the eyes like a brick of sunshine. But it wasn't the sunshine that made my head hurt; it was the golf ball behind my ear. I rubbed it and, like a crystal ball, visions began to appear. And Bill Jamison was in every one. I wasn't totally certain how I was going to handle my confrontation with Jamison. I'd seen him commit a felony—or at least pick up the money involved in a felony. That alone would be enough to make him act snotty.

I was driving up Sunset just about a half mile east of Beverly Glen. The tennis courts and wall-enclosed estates seemed peaceful and reassuring. Certainly in such a setting there was no place for crude violence. It was more the setting for veiled threats and sophisticated violence. But Jamison wasn't the sophisticated type. I was hoping he wasn't planning to spoil the mood of the neighborhood.

But I had the distinct feeling that Jamison had a point beyond which, if I chose to go, violence was a well-used option. Telling him I could link him to a kidnapping seemed to me to qualify as iffy territory. I didn't bring my gun, but I was smart. Or at least that's what I told myself. If I was so smart, why was I . . .? Oh, hell, I didn't want to start that one again.

I parked my car in front of the house that fronted Jamison's cottage. I could see a car further up the driveway that stopped in front of Jamison's apartment. I heard music coming from an open window. I climbed the same stairs I'd climbed a couple of days before when I'd discovered a naked woman hiding in Jamison's closet. Since then I'd taken to opening my own closet doors with some expectation. The closest I came to a repeat of the prize in Jamison's closet was a magazine with a picture of a naked woman in it.

I knocked on Jamison's door. No answer. I knocked again—still no answer. A few things crossed my mind. If Jamison were desperate and waiting for me inside, he might just blow me away, or stab me, or any number of gruesome possibilities. The music was still playing; it was a radio; I heard a commercial.

"Jamison! It's Ace Carpenter. I'd like to talk with you."

Still I heard nothing from behind the door except a voice telling me about an antiperspirant. I could have used it then; sweat was dripping from my armpits like water from a ceiling about to collapse from a heavy rain.

I could have just walked away, called Eddy, and had him take the risk. But, like I said, I'm a smart guy. I turned the doorknob. The door was unlocked. I pushed it open and stood to one side of the door. No shots flew out at me and no blades parted my hair. Cautiously I peered around the door frame into Jamison's apartment. No sign of movement. I stepped inside and closed the door behind me. There was the usual clutter of an unkempt bachelor, but beyond that there was nothing out of the ordinary—at least on such a cursory inspection.

I checked the closet again. No nude women. The bathroom door was closed. I moved to it and opened it.

There was Jamison, eyes open, staring at a place we'll all see one day, sitting in a pool of his own blood. His throat had been cut and the tub drain closed or clogged. I'd never seen that much blood before and I fell, more than a little nauseous, against the door frame and tried to talk my last meal into staying with me a little longer.

Eddy was there in less than fifteen minutes. He and his men didn't seem phased by the body swimming in its own blood. It was as though they were plumbers answering a call to fix a bad pipe. But I'd seen Jamison without that mannequin glare in his eyes. He had been alive. Now he was just so much evidence to be hauled away in a rubber bag.

"You OK, Ace?"

"Yeah, Eddy . . . well, no, not really. But I'll be all right."

"You ever see a stiff before?"

"Yeah, but not like that."

"Yeah, that's tough." But it wasn't tough for Eddy. I wondered what changes someone had to go through, what one had to see, before it wasn't tough anymore. With luck, I'd never know.

"I've got a theory," said Eddy finally. As much as

anything else, he was trying to help me focus on something other than Jamison's dead body.

"I'm listening."

"Let's make the assumption that whoever hit you was working with Jamison."

"OK."

"Naturally, he saw you get a peek at Jamison."

"OK."

"Now, according to your own estimations, Jamison might have been a punk of the highest order, but he wasn't a big-time criminal."

"OK."

"Now let's look at it from the point of view of his accomplice—the guy who put you to sleep. He knows you saw Jamison. You're a PI trying to nab the kidnappers. He and Jamison are the kidnappers. You saw Jamison, recognized him, and will probably be putting the screws to him. And if you do, the criminally unsophisticated Jamison could be pressured into pointing the finger to his partner. So, his partner decides to take matters into his own hands. Hence, what has taken place here today," said Eddy, as if he were conducting a class.

"Makes sense."

"Damn right it does."

"But what about Kathy St. John? This is bound to complicate getting her back."

"If they've even got her."

"What do you mean?"

"I'm betting even money that this whole job was just a scam dreamed up to take advantage of her disappearance. Besides, the other partner came over here and offed Jamison. So where was the girl?"

"Three possibilities," I said. "One, she was tied up or otherwise confined so that she could not escape. Two, there are more than two people involved. Three, they killed her already."

"Yeah. Well, we should know more when and if St. John is contacted again."

"They said no police."

"Too late now, Ace. But we'll be cool. We've been down this road a million times. You and St. John are amateurs. I'll contact St. John myself later today and explain the situation to him. We'll get a tap on his line within a few hours. In fact, that's already underway."

"OK. You're right."

"You up to a little interview?"

"Huh?"

"I'd like to talk with the lady in the house up front. Maybe she heard something. Want to come?"

"Yeah, let's go."

The woman in the front house turned out to be Mrs. Abe Greene, ten years widowed. Of course, she had observed all the commotion going on in her backyard and was more than anxious to talk with Eddy and me about Bill Jamison. So anxious, in fact, that she turned down the sound on one of her soap operas and only occasionally did she glance out of the corner of her eye to see what was almost happening. After we introduced ourselves and refused an offer of coffee, tea, or milk, Eddy began the questioning.

"Mrs. Greene, did you hear anything unusual last night or this morning coming from Bill Jamison's apartment above the garage?"

"There's always that damn music. It would drown out a bomb blast. I do believe he's getting more and more deaf and he has to turn the music up louder to even hear it."

Eddy and I looked at each other to acknowledge that what we might be getting from Mrs. Greene would be rather subjective material.

"Anything besides the music?"

She thought a minute, and then her eyebrows raised a

little. "I do remember something. Every night about 11:30, right after the news . . . Channel 7—I really like Cindy Landis . . . isn't she just a darling girl? You can believe what she has to say; not like Abner Klein. His eyes . . ."

"About 11:30?" Eddy asked, as if to remind her what planet she was on.

"Ah, well, yes, about that time every night, just after the Channel 7 news, I let Arthur out to do his business."

Seeing Mrs. Greene and hearing her, I considered the possibility that Arthur might be a man.

"Your pet?" asked Eddy.

"My dachshund. Here, Arthur," she cackled. Sure enough the dachshund came dragging his chest out of a room and into the living room where we were talking. He was old, maybe prematurely gray, and looked very sad. Mrs. Greene scooped him up with apparently no regard for his body and the way it bent and didn't bend. The dog remained impassive and came to rest on the woman's lap.

"Say hello, Arthur," she said, her head bowed over the dog's head. Strangely, Eddy and I seemed to be waiting for a response.

"Hello, boys," said Mrs. Greene out of the corner of her mouth, playing ventriloquist. As she did so, she moved one of the dog's paws in a sweeping manner to make it seem as if the dog was greeting us.

"Mrs. Greene, what did you hear or see when you let Arthur out to take a . . ."

"Do his business?" I finished Eddy's lingering sentence.

"I saw a little white foreign car."

"What was the make?"

"A Toyota or a Datsun. They look so much alike, I really can't tell the difference."

"Do you know who that car belonged to?"

"I don't know his name, but I've seen him hanging around often enough lately that I'm sure I can give you a description."

Eddy took out his notebook and flipped over the cover and a few used pages to a clean page.

"I'm ready," he said.

"He looked a good deal older than Mr. Jamison."

"About how old would that be?"

"I'd say his late forties or early fifties. He was balding and the hair he had left was gray. And he had a moustache. That was gray, too."

As she spoke I found myself thanking the powers that be that Mrs. Greene was not my neighbor.

"Anything else?" said Eddy, after the lady seemed to run out of gas.

"Well, there is something else, but I'm not sure it's my place to say it."

She waited long enough for Eddy to say something to serve as salve for her conscience. But it was a small abrasion and it didn't need much first aid.

"Anything you say, Mrs. Greene, could be of help. I'll be the final judge of what I can and cannot use. There's been a murder here and I'm going to need all the help I can get."

The word murder did a funny thing to her face. It didn't sting her the way I thought it would. It seemed to stimulate, excite her. Much like a soap opera coming to real life. After all, she didn't have to see the reality of it. Hers was a TV world. And being out of contact with the real world, she wasn't hurt by it, didn't feel the acute pain of life as it was lived by others. Her window on the world came complete with an on/off switch.

"Well, there *was* something else about the man in the white car. The way he walked and held his head and hands."

This baffled Eddy and me for an instant. Then we

both got the picture about the same time.

"You mean you believe that the man was a homosexual?"

"Yes," she said, trying to fake a little embarrassment.

"Did you hear anything last night out of the ordinary —above the music?"

"I believe I heard loud voices, like two people arguing."

"Were those two people the man from the white car and Bill Jamison?"

"I believe so. I couldn't be totally certain with the music going and all, but it makes sense doesn't it?"

Eddy wisely didn't bother to answer her question.

"When did the car leave?"

"About 1:00 A.M. I know that because I stayed up last night to watch the *Tonight Show*. You know who the host was last night?"

"No," said Eddy. "Who?"

"Johnny Carson," she said, almost incredulously. "I like him. Whenever he's on I like to watch the show. So, anyway, just as Dr. Joyce Brothers was finishing up talking about how to keep your marriage together, I heard a car zoom past my side window."

"Zoom?"

"Oh, yes. Just bolted out of here. Now, since Dr. Brothers was the last guest on the show, it must have been just before 1:00 A.M.—"

"That's very good, Mrs. Greene," said Eddy. He meant it. She had given him a lot to go on. Now all he had to do was find the guy with the white car.

And I could give Eddy the address of the man he was looking for right off the top of my head.

It took us about three hours to get a Ramey warrant, so it was midafternoon by the time Eddy and I, followed by a couple black and whites, rolled up in front of Everett Gray's Echo Park apartment house. Eddy and I spotted the white Toyota about the same time. He deployed his men and they surrounded the building.

Mrs. Greene's description had matched my recollection of Gray perfectly. Added to that was the fact that I'd seen him go into the Coastal Cruiser the night I'd visited Jamison there, so I was sure I had a winning combination.

When Gray opened the door he had on more clothes than the last time I'd called on him. But then the sun wasn't shining today and Gray didn't look in too good a mood. He looked as though he expected us, but the actuality of the event still surprised him—kind of like being served divorce papers after a long separation.

He tried on a smile, but it didn't fit.

"Come in," he said simply.

We entered and Eddy read Gray his rights.

"What is this all about?" Gray said it like an out-of-work actor who deserved to be.

"You are being sought in connection with the murder of Bill Jamison," said Eddy, as though he were just chatting with Gray about the color of his couch. It was lavender. I'm sorry, but it's true.

"William murdered! My God!" screamed Gray, his eyes nearly bulging out of their sockets. If he was putting on a show, I'd have to give him a good review. "I didn't kill William. You must believe me! I didn't!" he pleaded.

"We don't *have* to believe you, Mr. Gray," said Eddy. "We know that you were at Jamison's apartment until quite late last night. And that you had an argument with him loud enough so that the neighbors noticed. Further, we know that Jamison was mixed up in a kidnap scheme involving Kathy St. John."

Some of the surprise drained from Gray's eyes. He looked around the room, like a dying man looking for God for the first time.

"OK, OK," said Gray desperately. "William and I

were involved with the kidnap scheme. But that's it. I swear it."

"I'm afraid it isn't that simple," said Eddy.

"So it's you who's responsible for my headache," I said.

"I'm sorry. I was watching the pickup site from another building. I saw you circle around, go into a building, and take up a position to see who picked up the money. I was hoping I knocked you out before you saw William. I had to do it. But I'm not a murderer. Honestly."

I thought about asking him to cross his heart and hope to die, but decided against it.

"So where's Kathy?" I asked.

"We never had her."

"How do we know you haven't put her someplace where she'll never be found?"

"What do you mean . . . Oh, my God, no! I swear to God, we never had her. Jesus, William and I aren't killers. My God, no!" said Gray, kind of winding down like a doll that, when wound up, pleads and whimpers a lot.

"You and Jamison told St. John you had his daughter," said Eddy.

"Yeah, but that was just a way to make a quick twenty-five thousand dollars.

Although I didn't say it at the time, it fit with what both St. John and I had agreed upon. Neither Jamison nor Gray were big-time. They were opportunists. They took their shot, but it didn't hit anything. Except a bullseye full of trouble.

"Tell us about last night," said Eddy. As he did, he snapped his fingers in the direction of a blond cop standing in the open doorway. The cop came to him, bent down, and listened as Eddy spoke softly to him. The blond cop took out a notepad and sat down with the three of us to make a fourth, in case we all got bored and decided to play bridge.

"You're right," said Gray, as if trying to assuage Eddy a little. "I *was* at William's house last night. I got there about 10:00, maybe 10:30."

"Why did you go to Jamison's place last night?"

"Part of it you know."

"I want you to put it in your own words."

"Well, as you know," began Gray, settling like the earth after an eight-point quake, "William was seen yesterday—by you, Mr. Carpenter—when he picked up the money. I went to tell him that he had been seen and that we'd better get the hell out of town before we both got picked up. We were both in on it," said Gray directly to Eddy, "so why would I want to kill him?"

Gray knew the answer to that question as well as we did, but he just wanted to see if we were awake.

"That's obvious. Jamison was seen, not you. The only one who could link you to the felony was Bill Jamison. Seems like a crystal clear motive to me. How 'bout you?"

Gray winced his eyes closed and began to massage them with the thumb and forefinger of his right hand, resting his right elbow on his knee. Finally he laid his face in both open palms and dragged his head to an upright position, facing us. He seemed to have aged before our eyes.

"Hey, I know it looks bad, but I'm telling you the truth."

"What time did you leave last night?"

"I don't know, but it was about 1:30 A.M. when I got home."

That checked with Mrs. Greene's account.

"But I swear that he was alive when I left. I swear it!"

Too bad for Gray a person's word meant so little.

"How would you characterize your conversation with Jamison last night?"

"I know this probably won't help my cause any, but I'm telling you the truth and I'm holding nothing back," he prefaced. "William wanted to continue with our plan and get another twenty-five thousand out of St. John. He said that since St. John blew it—by sending Ace here, who decided to get cute—that we were entitled to some more cash."

"Didn't that sound dangerous to him since Ace had seen him?"

"He said that he would go to a motel later that night, after I left. And with the extra twenty-five thousand we could both leave the country until the whole thing blew over. Or maybe even never come back. But I'd lost my nerve. I was ready to take the money and run."

"What did Jamison say when you wanted to pull out?"

"He became violent, threatening. He said that we were both in the thing until the end. And the end would come when we had our second payment. All right, I was angry; scared more than angry. But I know William, and when his mind is made up—especially when money is concerned—there's no talking to him."

We were all silent for a few seconds, then Eddy asked the question I'd been wanting to ask.

"OK, let's say we buy your story about not having kidnapped the St. John girl—which I may or may not be taking an option on—how did you know you could get away with it?"

"What do you mean?"

"You get coy with me and I'll have you put through a few paces that aren't on the regular agenda." That sounded cute, but Eddy looked as hard as frozen steel when he said it and it made Gray a contestant with all the answers.

"Sure, sure, OK. You know that William is—or was —Kathy's boyfriend. They were close, real close. Kathy had had a bad time recently, with that Smith murder and all, so she decided to take off for a week or two. She told William she was going north for a while."

"North? That could be Bakersfield or the North Pole. Put some meat on the bones, Gray."

Everett Gray was visibly shaking now. "Honest to God, I don't know. That's all he told me."

"Think very hard. *Very* hard."

"Ok, OK. I'm not real sure, but I thought he said something that made me think she was headed for the Bay Area. I don't know exactly where, but he said something about San Francisco. I swear that's all I know."

"She gonna stay with friends? Rent a cottage? What?"

"I don't know. Really, I don't. Let me think if there's anything. Give me a second." Gray began to rub his forehead with the tips of his fingers as if trying to squeeze information out of his head. "No, nothing. Maybe, well, yes, I think he said she was going to stay in a hotel in San Francisco. But that's it. William said she wouldn't be back for a week or so."

"So how did the bright idea of faking the kidnapping come up?"

"William knew Kathy didn't like her father. And what was twenty-five thousand dollars to him anyhow? Kathy told William that her father often lost that much when he went to Vegas, which he did about once a month. Anyhow, William told me one of the reasons Kathy left was that she was going through some personal problems, something involving her father. She didn't want to talk with her father until she had it all sorted out. So William thought sure we'd be OK if we wrapped the whole thing up in a few days. That's it. That's all of it. I swear."

"Not quite all. Jamison was killed last night. OK,

that's all for now," said Eddy. He motioned for a Chicano uniformed officer who was standing in the doorway to come in.

"Take Mr. Gray downtown and book him on a 181 PC, suspicion of murder."

Gray didn't even resist. He was a decimated man. The cop followed him into his bedroom, where Gray grabbed a jacket and a couple of books. Then he was led away, head down—a body animated only by another's will.

"How about a late lunch?" I asked Eddy.

"You buyin'?"

"Maybe."

"I might be interested."

We danced like this for a few minutes and finally decided on Dutch treat at a restaurant we each could afford only if we each were paying for one person.

After we were seated and had ordered meals worthy of a day's work well done, Eddy disappeared to make a phone call. I sipped on a Stolichnaya and watched a dark-haired waitress with particularly good-looking legs bending over, exposing the backs of two sumptuous upper thighs as she took an order. She looked as though she could give any man an appetite.

Eddy returned just as the salad was being served.

"So what do you think?" he said.

"About what?"

"House dressing or Thousand Island." Both had been set in a silver service between us.

"I'm a Thousand Island man, myself. But you look like house dressing, house wine, house anything to me, Eddy."

"You're right," he said cheerfully, not taking it as a slam. It wasn't. It's no insult to accuse a factory worker of watching the football game on Sunday while knocking down a couple of beers. It was probably the truth. And a truth he was comfortable with.

"You believe Gray?" said Eddy, after liberally showering his vegetables with an oil and vinegar mixture.

I thought about it a minute before I answered. "I know this sounds crazy, but I do."

"Hmmm," was Eddy's reply. "Why?"

"I don't know really. Just my take on it, I guess. I should be happy if they break his neck," I said, rubbing the back of my head. "Gray's an asshole, but I don't think he's a murderer."

"If he had hit you a little harder, he might have killed you."

"What do you think?" I asked after I'd tasted the Thousand Island. I stuck some salad in the stuff just to add flavor.

"I think you're right."

That was a surprise.

"Why?"

"Just a hunch."

Eddy was not one for hunches. Knowing Eddy, he was usually ready to accept the most logical explanation, regardless of proof. Most times he was right.

"Bull," I said, scooping up some more Thousand Island. I ate my salads with a spoon, not a fork.

Eddy got a smile on his face. "I just talked with Casper downtown. Jamison wasn't killed until at least five this morning. And that's the soonest. One, two, even three this morning is impossible, he says."

"So Gray isn't our man after all."

"Probably not. Sure, he could have come back later, but I don't think so. We're dropping the 181, but Gray's still on ice for his part in the kidnapping plot to fleece St. John. Funny part about that is that if Jamison's nosy neighbor hadn't been so nosy, Gray might never have even been popped for anything."

"Maybe, maybe not. So where does that leave us?"

"Who would want Jamison dead? Who has a motive?"

I thought about it and spooned the last of my Thousand Island from my bowl. Looking Eddy in the eye, I said, "St. John."

"Makes sense," he said, as if it were old news. "If *you* found out about Jamison, maybe St. John did, too. He's a powerful man and he's got eyes and ears everywhere; paid eyes and ears. So maybe we should find out where St. John was last night."

"Probably pretty visible, I'd guess," I said. "St. John wouldn't kill anyone himself."

"You're right," agreed Eddy, as our main dishes were delivered by the leggy brunette. She'd heard the word kill when she'd arrived and she looked uneasy.

"It's all right," I said appeasingly. "He's a cop." She smiled as if that made it all right. The talk became more sparse as I dug into the scalloped oysters and a fresh turbot. Eddy began to sculpt the lean meat in front of him into bite-sized pieces, adorning each with a generous amount of steak sauce.

"The boys done over at Jamison's?" I asked.

"Yep. And Casper relayed a message."

"About the money?"

"You're sharp, Ace. You should be a detective. It's not there. Not at Gray's, either."

"That could mean a couple things. Jamison or Gray put it somewhere, or whoever offed Jamison took it."

"Find Jamison's killer and you find the money," said Eddy, as if it could be no other way.

We talked a bit more about Gray and St. John and their longtime animosity.

Finally I said, "I'm gonna be pretty busy the next couple of days. I'm heading out of town. But I'll keep in touch."

"Going to San Francisco?" asked Eddy, sipping at his coffee.

"That's right."

"Better have more to go on than what Gray said. San Francisco's a big place."

"So I hear."

"You're not holding out on me, now, are you, Ace?"

"Now, Eddy, do I ever hold out on you?"

"Sure, that's why I asked."

"I just don't want you spinning your wheels on something meaningless. If what I have has any teeth, I'll let you tame it, OK?"

He just smiled. We each picked up our check and headed for the door.

At the cash register I handed over a ten and a five to cover my check. Eddy handed the cashier a five and got some change back. I was about to ask a stupid question when the cashier said, "Thank you, Sergeant Price, and have a good day."

After I got home and packed enough clothes for a couple of nights, I called Eddy at the West L.A. station. He gave me Edward Smith's home address from the fact sheet on him.

"Give me a call tomorrow night, OK, Ace?"

"I'll call you as soon as anything pays off. Don't worry. I've got my mittens clipped to my coatsleeves."

San Francisco's a beautiful place. The cable cars, the Victorian buildings, with their faces hand-toweled clean each day by the thick, wet fog. On one level San Francisco was rich, elegant. It was a city. A real city. Los Angeles was a series of suburbs, a bunch of small cities tied together in more of an alphabetical than a cultural order. New York was a city. Chicago—as much as I personally disliked it—was a city. And San Francisco was a city. Indeed, the most beautiful by any sane standard.

But there was another level to San Francisco. A level that had not escaped the notice of the country, and the

world, for that matter. Mayors were murdered by other
government officials. Presidents were shot at in San
Francisco. The Tenderloin District was notorious for
prostitution and a hell of a lot more. Bizarre cults were
as common as a Presbyterian church would be in the
Midwest. San Francisco was one crazy place.

I checked into acceptable lodgings on Geary in the
heart of downtown. It was a room with a view—of another hotel across the street.

I set my bag down on the bed and called Sergeant
Clegg of the S.F.P.D. He was a friend of Eddy's, and
Eddy had said Clegg would be willing to do a "very
small" favor for me if I mentioned Eddy's name. I gave
Sergeant Clegg the San Francisco phone number I'd
found on Kathy St. John's notepad. He promised to
match it up with an address from their "backwards
book" in an hour or so. I gave him my number at the
hotel and went out for a bite to eat.

I took a taxi to Union, where there was always a lot
of action. Clubs, restaurants, shops—it was a busy
place. I'd remembered it from the few times I'd been to
Frisco.

I chose a place called the Golden Gate Pub. It had an
old world ambience and the cutest waitresses with the
least attire.

My waitress was an Oriental. I'd seen a lot of Oriental
women since I'd arrived in the Bay Area. Each one made
me think of Jenny. It's funny how you miss someone
when you can't touch them. It was an old story, but I
began to think a lot about Jenny and why the hell we
didn't put our relationship on track. And how maybe
she didn't know exactly how I felt about her. But that
was loneliness talking, I told myself, and dug into the
fresh crab that had just been delivered.

Over a nice Chenin blanc and the excellent seafood, I
pondered my position in this foreign territory. Gray had
said that Kathy was in the Bay Area, probably some

hotel in San Francisco. Edward Smith used to live, according to my information from Eddy, on a houseboat in Sausalito. It was my educated guess that the address I was going to get from Sergeant Clegg and Smith's address would be identical. For some reason, Smith had wanted Kathy St. John to call his wife. Why, I had no idea. But I figured I'd go sniff around the Smith houseboat for a couple of days and see what I could see. Maybe Kathy would just walk onto the scene, but even *I* wasn't that much of an optimist. I didn't want to tell Eddy because he'd be duty-bound to dispatch men to the Smith residence, and that might scare off Kathy for good. After all, my job, what I was being paid to do, was to find Kathy St. John. I'd give Eddy anything I found, but I reserved the right to follow my hunches first.

When I got back to the hotel a message was waiting for me. Sergeant Clegg had called and left a number.

"Got that address for ya, Carpenter," said Clegg when I finally got him on the line.

"I'm ready. Shoot."

"It's a houseboat in Sausalito. The *Picadilly,* slip fourteen. Any good?"

"Sounds like a winner. And thanks a lot. I'll tell Eddy you were a big help."

"OK. And you can tell Eddy to go to hell," replied Clegg good-naturedly.

"He's been told that so many times, I'm sure he knows the way." Clegg thought that was funny enough to laugh in my ear. I was grateful enough to listen.

We made small talk for a few minutes about Eddy and a couple of other people we both knew, and then he extended the obligatory we'll-have-to-get-together line, which neither one of us grabbed hold of.

It was about 9:30 P.M. by the time I'd showered and gotten squared away. The color TV didn't work, so I decided to take a walk. I went down to the Tenderloin District on Broadway. It was a sexual smorgasbord.

Neon women flashed off and on for my attention and money. Men grabbed my arm as I passed their particular establishments and gave me their spiel about how my cash would be wasted anywhere in the city but "right here, man." I was ready to waste some money, but I was determined to be quite careful about how I was to be duped.

"Wrestle a naked woman?" No. "Fantasy Fulfillment" read a sign over a woman with high heels and shoulder chains. "The Only Bottomless Show in Town" read another. "50D and Firm" offered more of a believe-it-or-not type of show. There was another place where I could talk to a girl on the other side of a glass wall. From the PR, it sounded like she would be nude and willing to do provocative things for me as we talked. The more I "tipped," the more provocative she was willing to be.

Then I saw it. The oasis in the sea of sex was a sign that depicted two women throwing each other about in a ring full of mud. The hawker made it sound like the Olympics, so I let him pick my pocket of seven dollars. I was led to a table near the ring where I was given what appeared to be a large bib. A waitress came over to me —the service was fast because there were only about a half dozen guys in the place besides me—and informed me of the two-drink minimum.

"I wasn't told about a minimum at the door," I said to the scantily clad barmaid, who, I could tell from the dried mud on her elbow, doubled as a wrestler.

"That's not my problem," she said coldly. "Order or leave."

It wasn't a brilliant patchwork of possibilities. Especially because I was already out seven bucks.

"OK, OK. I'll take a beer. That's got to be cheaper than a mixed drink."

"All drinks are three-fifty. Beers, mixed drinks, all the same price," she said, as if for the umpteenth time.

"What's the strongest drink in the house?" I asked.

"I don't drink. Alcohol is for idiots," she proclaimed, not looking at me, staring off into space.

Now she had me. If I didn't drink, I'd have to leave. If I did drink I would be initiated into Idiots Club.

"Could I give you the money for two drinks and not drink?"

"That's pretty stupid, ain't it?" She looked me in the face to deliver this evaluation.

"OK, I'll have a Stolichnaya on the rocks."

She laughed as though I'd just told a joke. But then she wasn't the kind of girl to laugh *with* you.

"Does this look like the kind of place that would have expensive vodka?" she asked rhetorically. Again she gave me the benefit of her condescending gaze.

I wanted to tell her just what the place looked like, but the waitress didn't look like she'd take criticism well.

"I'll take a gin and tonic." For me that was always a good standby drink.

"Great. You want them both now, or one at a time?"

"One at a time." I realized it would be less work for her if she brought them both at once, and she could tell that two was definitely going to be my limit.

"May I smoke in here?" I asked. I had noticed that no one else was smoking.

"You can set yourself on fire as far as I'm concerned," she said, this time to the ceiling again. Then she turned to walk away. Her buttocks were a little large and didn't quite fit into her bikini briefs. The excess seemed to knead itself as she walked away through two red swinging doors.

I took out my tobacco pouch, filled my pipe, tampered the filling into readiness, and lit a savory bowl of Tropical Mix.

After about five minutes, two women who looked less like Amazons than massage parlor refugees stepped into the ring looking more bored than antagonistic. At least with professional wrestling there was a hint of show-manship. One girl was black and stood about five feet five, the other girl was Mexican, a little shorter and stouter. Both were wearing bikinis, the Mexican opting for a more modest version because of her more hefty figure.

My waitress rang a bell next to the ring as she delivered two drinks to a fellow who was nearly asleep sitting about three tables to my left. His eyes jerked open in alarm when the bell rang, and he instinctively started to get up out of his seat and look around for God knows what. He rubbed his eyes and sat down to watch the women, who were now wrestling a few feet away.

The black girl threw the Mexican girl over her shoulder and the latter came splashing down in the mud, sending a glob of soggy brown earth in the direction of the guy who had just awakened. It hit him squarely in the forehead and dripped down over his plastic, see-through bib.

About halfway through the first five minutes, the black girl removed the other girl's halter top, to the reaction of no one. From that moment forward the Mexican girl was at a decided disadvantage in that whenever she gained an advantage on the black girl, the latter would simply reach around and squeeze the Mexican girl's nipples. I had the feeling the whole affair was as choreographed as an Andy Williams Christmas Show dance number, but everyone seemed to get what they expected. Nothing.

The match finally ended when the black girl removed the Mexican girl's bikini bottom and positioned her in a not-too-ladylike submission hold. I got the distinct feeling the time limit had simply expired.

I figured that if you saw one of these matches, you'd seen them all, so I decided to just leave my money for the second drink and take off. Besides, this was not the ideal atmosphere in which to sort out my thoughts. So I left the Tenderloin District, which I can only describe as a lower chakra gone berserk.

I passed an open rent-a-car agency on the way back to the hotel. There had been enough gin in my drinks at the mud arena to get me drunk only if I hadn't eaten for about a year, so I was still wide awake. I had planned to rent a car in the morning, but, since the rate would end up being the same anyhow, and since I was alert, I decided to go to work instead of to bed.

The drive across the Golden Gate Bridge at night was spectacular. San Francisco looked like a magic place fading seductively in and out of view through the light fog.

I took the first right past the bridge and followed about a mile and half of winding road down into Sausalito. I parked my car on the main street in front of an antique shop and found my way to a local watering hole and ordered a Stolichnaya. Nobody laughed when I did.

The Blue Anchor Saloon looked just like saloons looked in John Wayne movies. There were large mirrors behind the bar and on two other walls. There was even a picture of a naked lady behind the bar next to the mirror. However, instead of the typical rotund, pink cherubim usually seen in the movie version, this picture was a photograph and the lady's pose was more indicative of *Penthouse* magazine than the Old West.

An old fan was motionless overhead, as warm, summer afternoons had given way to chilly autumn nights. I took my place at the bar. The establishment was about a quarter full.

"Hi," I said to the bartender. He looked to be in his early thirties, was bearded and casually dressed with an old-fashioned white shirt and black vest. He was also a few pounds overweight, which probably was why his vest had been left open.

"Howdy," he said, not the way a cowboy would say it, but the way it came to be said by longhairs of the late sixties and early seventies. "Haven't seen you here before."

"No. Just visiting San Francisco from L.A. My name's Tom Carson," I lied.

"So what brings you into Sausalito?"

"Edward Smith," I said as noncommittally as possible. I could tell by whatever expression he would flash me what tack to take next.

He raised his eyebrows in such a way as to let me know where he stood. If he had warmed to the name, I'd have had to play at being spiritual. It was not my best impression. Fortunately his demeanor when I mentioned the name indicated his anti-Smith point of view.

"I'm a writer," I said. "Don't know much about him, really."

"What magazine?"

"Freelancing for *Rolling Stone.*" I imagined he inferred that I was a gonzo journalist and that his name might appear in what might eventually be called "Fear and Loathing in Sausalito." Anyhow, he smiled at me, bobbed his head, and said some nice things about *Rolling Stone* magazine.

"You ever meet Smith?" I asked.

"This on the record?" he asked, drying a glass with a stained white towel.

"Kind of. I won't quote you directly—unless you want me to."

"No siree. I've got to live here. Smith was pretty well thought of here."

"I take it that what you might have to say wouldn't be appreciated by his admirers."

"You might say that."

"Where does Mrs. Smith live?"

"Houseboat about two blocks down, slip fourteen.

It's kind of rustic-looking. It has wood paneling on the outside and there's a lion, like the Trafalgar Square lions, sitting out front."

"So what makes Smith a badman in your eyes?"

"Hell, it's not that he was a bad guy—it's just that I don't like anybody being treated like a saint."

"What about Mrs. Smith?"

"She's all right. She's been in here a few times."

"By herself?"

"Just because she comes in here with somebody doesn't mean anything in my book. She never came in here and made a scene. Nice lady. Won't say anything bad about her. On *or* off the record."

"That's understandable, her coming in here. Nice place," I said. "And Edward was out of town so much. No big deal." I tried to smooth his feathers. "How long have the Smiths lived here?"

"Ever since they came here from England, the way I hear it."

"How long have you been in Sausalito?"

"Just a couple years. I'm from Portland."

"Anybody in town here who could set me straight on the Smiths? Anyone willing to talk?"

Just then someone ordered a drink and he went away thinking about my question. After he'd poured an Anchor Steam into a frosted mug, he returned.

"Allie Graham. She lives up in the hills. She's been friends with the Smiths ever since they arrived. In fact, Helen Smith often goes over to Allie's for tea and coffee in the afternoon."

"If they're that close, she might not talk."

"Allie's close with everyone who's anyone in Sausalito. She has afternoon teas with writers, painters, poets, musicians, politicians, you name it. She's the Gertrude Stein of the Bay Area. Loves to talk. She's in her seventies now. Witty, lucid, a real trip. You don't need an appointment, either. Her door is always open after about ten in the morning. She also writes a column, kind of a cross between *People* and a gossip column, about Bay Area notables. Yeah, she's the one. If there's anything to be known, she knows it."

"But will she tell?"

"That I don't know."

I finished my Stolichnaya and hit the streets. The fog was thicker now and I could feel the dampness on my moustache. I could hear a foghorn somewhere in the distance blowing an eerie tune and the smell of fish filled my nostrils. The water lapped against the cement embankment I was walking beside on my way to the Smith houseboat. As the smells, sights, and sounds filled my senses, pictures filled my mind. Pictures of Kathy St. John taking a bullet in her apartment. Pictures I'd seen of Edward Smith lying dead in his limousine. Pictures of Bill Jamison bathing in his own blood. It was like being in a dark room with a killer—I could hear the bodies falling, but I couldn't see a thing—not even a gun pointed at my head.

I felt alone and vulnerable as I stood in front of the lion that marked the houseboat the bartender said was owned by the Smiths.

There was a light on in the room nearest me. I just kept walking and, about four houseboats on, doubled back and took up a position about thirty yards from the Smith residence. I was in shadows and fog, so I was almost totally concealed. I wasn't certain how long I was willing to wait, nor, for that matter, what I was waiting for.

It was coming up on 11:30 and I was thinking seriously about getting back to my warm hotel bed when a door opened on the boat and two figures stood illuminated in the doorway. A yellow shock of light cut the darkness and dispersed in the fog. The woman, though I had no way of identifying her, was probably Helen Smith. The man I recognized. He was Simon Bernstein.

I crept a little closer and ducked behind a car, which could not have been more than twelve feet away from where Bernstein and the woman were talking. I could just make out what they were saying.

"All right, Helen. I know that none of this is easy. But I believe you have made the right decision, and I will do my best to help you follow through with it."

"I hope so, Simon. It's the end of a long road."

"Of course, but the whole thing is now up to her. You must remember that, Helen."

"I know. Look, Simon, it's quite late. I think we've about talked this thing to death."

"I agree. I'll pick you up tomorrow evening at about seven. Now you get some rest."

"OK. Good night, Simon," said the woman, and shut the door. There was nearly total blackness again. Bernstein opened the driver's side door to the car I was hiding behind. I dove away from it and retreated to a pile of cement bricks a few yards away.

Bernstein drove off. The light in the houseboat went black.

I walked back through the fog to my car. As I drove across the Golden Gate Bridge, San Francisco was now completely obscured by a rolling, smoky wetness. I needed to get some sleep. I had work to do the next day. For one thing, I had a date with Allie Graham. For another, I planned to be the third wheel in Bernstein and Helen Smith's seven o'clock rendezvous.

The next morning as I drove back into Sausalito the fog was starting to vanish into thin air. But from the access road into Sausalito only the tops of the downtown buildings were visible.

It was about 11:00 A.M. by the time I parked my car in a lot. An outdoor cafe, the Blue Dolphin, was serving breakfast. I grabbed a handful of depressing ink and paper from a corner vending machine and sat down at a table that provided a view that looked out onto the bay.

The news hinted of war. There were pictures of dead babies in their mothers' arms in Cambodia; a major auto company had just closed one of its biggest production plants in the Southland; a policeman had been shot while trying to break up a fight on a junior high campus; a religious group had begun a campaign to "feed the world" and to get it rolling was throwing a thousand-dollar-a-plate dinner. The only thing that kept my coffee from making an encore in a nearby restroom was the news that the Angels had acquired an ace left-hander from the Yankees. Now *that* was good news.

I ordered eggs and wheat toast from a waitress, who looked as though she had left a wake-up call that never came. I got most of my order, ate it while reading the sports section, and asked for the check.

"Excuse me," I said to the waitress. "Could you tell me how to get to Allie Graham's house?"

"I beg your pardon," she slurred, as if I'd just nudged her awake.

"Allie Graham's house. She lives around here."

"Oh, Allie. Sure. You can walk there from here." That didn't help much. I could have walked to China from there if I'd felt really ambitious.

"It's about four blocks. Just go out there," she said, pointing to the front door—that much I already knew—"turn left and then go right at the first street and just follow that street to the top of the first hill. On your right-hand side you'll see a green house with white trim sitting back a little off the road. That's Allie's. You an artist or something?"

"Yes," I said, certain that I was in fact something.

"Well, I do modeling," she said, shifting her weight to one side in a more promotional pose. "I'm cheap."

That I already knew.

The silence served as a positive response to her. "Ten

dollars an hour with clothes, fifteen without."

"Are you worth 50 percent more without your clothes?" I just couldn't help myself.

"Look at these tits," she said, dropping her head, looking at them herself. "I'm not even twenty-one yet," she said, as though it were a selling point. It wasn't. "And I've got good legs, too."

"I'm sure you do."

"You want my card?"

"Sure," I said. What could I say?

She disappeared for a minute and returned with her card in hand. It said that she did modeling, macrame, and taught modern dance. It didn't, however, mention her skills as a waitress. Just as well.

"Thank you very much," I said after reading the card and depositing it in my pocket. "If I need a model while I'm in San Francisco, I'll call you for sure." Again I was not lying. If I decided to take up painting and needed a model in the next day or two, I *would* call her. But then, the chances of that happening were about the same as my deciding to take up astrophysics and fly to Jupiter before returning to Los Angeles. But the important thing was that I was not lying.

I paid my check with some plastic money—better that than rubber checks—and began my walk up to Allie's. The sun was brilliant and the little town glistened as I made my way up the hill. The houses were much like the hillside houses in the Hollywood Hills. Some were on stilts. All had fabulous views of the bay and San Francisco.

I was puffing by the time I got to Allie's green house. A white-haired woman with a smile a good lifetime wide answered the door and, without asking me why I was standing there, ushered me in and offered me some tea, coffee, milk, or juice. I settled on some juice. Orange.

We made a little small talk about Sausalito, the beautiful day, and so on while she went to her refrigerator and poured me a glass of o.j.

"So what brings you to my door, young man?" she asked as she sat down in a large winged chair opposite a similar one in which I was now comfortably entrenched.

"Well, you see, I'm a writer for, actually a freelance writer for, *Rolling Stone* and . . ."

"A stringer then."

"A what?"

She chuckled lightly. "Continue."

"Well, I'm on assignment to come up here and write a piece on Edward Smith."

"Ah, Edward," said Allie, sipping liquid from a cup. "Go on Mr. ah . . ."

"Carson. Tom Carson. Anyhow, I haven't formed any opinion as to the angle I'm going to take in the story. I'm just gathering information. Background information."

"I see. Well, anything I can do to be of help. I'll tell you anything you want to know. Would you like to take notes?"

"Of course," I said, a little surprised at her willingness to cooperate with a total stranger. I withdrew a pen and a pad from my coat pocket. "All set."

"Make sure you get this now, Mr. Carson. I'm going to establish my own credibility with your readers first."

"Good idea," I said. The old lady was playing into my hands.

"I'm from England, you know."

"No, I didn't."

"Oh, yes. I'm surprised you don't know. I'm rather well-known there, you see."

"Oh?"

"Why, yes. I'm the Queen of England. Don't you recognize me?"

I put down my pen and looked at her again. She was smiling at me.

"You're not the Queen of England," I said. I don't know why I said it. Looking back, it must have been obvious.

"And you're not who you say you are. If you're not telling me the truth, why should I tell *you* the truth?"

She had a point that was hard to debate. I looked hard at her again. There was a quality in those eyes I'd not seen often in my life. The only word I could think of that fits it was wisdom. That and a forgiving, disarming sense of humor that made her eyes twinkle and placed her mouth on the constant verge of a smile. I didn't have a prayer.

"OK," I said resignedly. I took my identification out of my pocket and handed it to her.

"Ace Carpenter, Private Detective. Kind of a strange name, Ace. I figured you for a PI," she said, handing my ID back to me.

"No kidding?"

"No kidding."

I liked Allie Graham.

"So what do you want to know?"

"Do you mean you'll still give me information?"

"If I don't think I should answer, I won't. You seem like a nice enough guy. Even if you are a liar. I imagine in your line of work, you call it working undercover. I'm sure you have it rationalized somehow."

I did. But she delivered the scolding so good-naturedly that it seemed to me that I'd just had a realization rather than assumed guilt.

I told her the story: Edward Smith's contact with Kathy, Kathy's disappearance, Jamison's murder. It took two more glasses of juice, but I was having a good time. So was Allie. She was on the edge of her seat.

"So you're up here because a kidnapper told you Kathy might be staying in a San Francisco hotel?"

"That and a hunch. I want to know why Smith put Kathy in touch with his wife. I want to know about

Smith. About his wife. Where did they come from? I just have the feeling that someone is holding back a key piece of information. It's like trying to piece together a jigsaw puzzle with one of the pieces in your pocket. Then again, I might be totally wrong."

"But then, you might be right," said Allie, ever the optimist. "So what do you want to know?"

"How long have you known the Smiths?"

"About five years. I got to know them shortly after they moved here."

"From where?"

"England."

"Honest?" I said, half-jokingly.

"Honest. Edward attended Oxford, or at least that's what a diploma in his office at home indicates."

"Do you have any reason to doubt its validity?"

"None whatsoever. Edward Smith, in my humble opinion, was a brilliant man. He may have become slightly infatuated with himself toward the end, but still not as much as persons in similar situations have done in the past. As far as I know, his and Helen's marriage was as stable as a rock—I just figured you would get around to that eventually."

"Yes, I would have. What about Helen's background?"

"Helen is a real lady. By that I mean she's not nouveau riche. She has money and she's comfortable with it, she doesn't flaunt it. You can sense that she is an educated, cultured woman."

"I see." I felt Allie's perceptions, though not the most objective, were probably more reliable than most eyewitness reports. Allie had an eye for people and a tongue able to communicate what she saw. I was in school.

"What else can you tell me about Helen?"

"I believe she's been ill recently. Before Edward's death. Maybe for the past year or so. She seems to be carrying some kind of burden inside her. I can tell, believe me."

I did.

"Her rather solemn demeanor is such a contrast to Edward's robots—that's what I call the people who run his centers. They treat Edward like a god."

"I know. I've met a couple of them."

"Silly, isn't it?"

"Yes."

"I think it actually embarrassed Edward. He's not, or he wasn't, a very social person. Very intelligent, witty, a wonderful dinner guest—always brought the best wine to be had in the city. But his friend Simon, well, that's another story."

"Simon Bernstein?" I asked.

"You've been working, I see."

"I try."

"Yes, Simon Bernstein. Simon, who's really not a bad fellow, is very ambitious. I think that it was he who got Edward involved in going into 'pop psychology.' Before that time, Edward was just another psychologist in the Bay Area. He was making good money, and was well-known in the field, but Simon talked him into giving fast-food-type self-help courses."

"Do you know Simon well?"

"Oh my, yes. With the Smiths and Simon being such good friends, Simon always tagged along to my parties."

"Which, I'm sure, were well-attended."

"I must admit I have a reputation for throwing a good party. They're not expensive. People *bring* most of the food and drink. I just provide the space."

"It's a nice space," I said sincerely, waxing slightly esoteric.

"Thank you."

"What about Helen's background? Where does she come from?"

"She lived with Edward in England when he was at Oxford."

"Did she work?"

"Never mentioned it."

"Was Edward working his way through Oxford?"

"Definitely not. He was a student about twenty-eight hours a day, to hear him tell it."

"Must have had some money saved. Did Edward tell you what he did before going to Oxford?"

"Not much vocationally. Part-time jobs, here and there to pay for school."

"Somebody must have had some money."

"My bet would be that Helen supported Edward while he was in school, but that's only a guess. Why don't you ask her?"

"I plan to. Oh, by the way, I trust you won't tell her I've been talking with you."

"I'm not going to lie to my friends."

"I'm not asking you to."

"I'm not going to call her and give her a report, if that's what you mean. If I see her in the street and she asked about you, I'll tell her. I haven't told you anything you couldn't find out from doing a little sniffing around on your own elsewhere. And I've not told you anything Helen or Edward would have wanted kept in confidence. But if a girl's life is in danger, I'll do what I can to help."

I couldn't hope for anything more.

"If you find something that has no bearing on finding the girl, let it lie," said Allie seriously.

I started to answer her in a glib manner, when my eyes locked with hers. She wanted a promise. I gave it to her without saying a word.

I still had most of the afternoon to kill, so I walked around Sausalito for a while. It was a wonderful place, the kind of place tourists tell their friends they'll retire to someday. Those days never come, but it helps to think they might.

I found a stairway leading from the sidewalk to the top of a hill about three flights up. I climbed two flights and sat down. I'd had the foresight and the appetite to purchase a cold beer and a ham and cheese sandwich at a deli that fronted the bay. I unwrapped the sandwich, screwed off the beer bottle cap, and feasted on some food and the beauty of Sausalito.

As I looked out over the peaceful water and laid-back tranquility of the little village, I pondered what I was about to do. Maybe my hunch was wrong. Maybe I was just half right and I'd be opening a can of worms that would simply hurt people for no reason.

I thought about me, my mind, the way I thought. In my line of work I was always dealing with people who lived as though there was no such thing as a lie, only gradients of the truth. And as a citizen of the world, I lived in a time in which people were educated but still pretty stupid, and the rulers manipulative and secure within the rationale that since people didn't know how to govern themselves, it was best left to professionals. The flaw was that the professionals were themselves either puppets or power-mad. The puppets were the politicians who looked at government and its issues simply as positive or negative PR, and were only available at election time. The power-mad were simply the worst and most dangerous of criminals. Endless talk of how to govern had totally replaced the act of doing the people's business. People had become statistics: votes for politicians, dollars for commerce. I used to think I was part of the game. But I was really just a hat on a monopoly board—a piece to be moved, but not a player. I, like most Americans, was tired of being manipulated, but couldn't think of anything to do about it.

It was this sense of being manipulated all the time that contributed to my conspiratorial mindset. I took for granted that any act of consequence by any intelligent person had at least two levels of reality. One, what was seen, the other what really happened. I saw in it everything. Sometimes I was wrong. I saw it in Kathy St. John's disappearance. I felt a sense of conspiracy, of cover-up.

As I finished my sandwich and beer I looked out again upon Sausalito and wondered what it would look like in ten years. The vision diseased my appetite.

I left a wake-up call at the desk for 4:30 and caught an afternoon nap. I dreamed about a man with a beard who was chasing Kathy St. John down Sunset Boulevard. She couldn't seem to hear him. She was looking for Bill Jamison, who was nowhere in sight. I could see him; he was lying behind a billboard floating in blood. But Kathy just kept calling his name. David St. John was skiing down the Hollywood Hills using two brown Mercedes, one on each foot, as skis. An Oriental, whose face I couldn't make out, was sitting on top of a restaurant roof and shooting people who roller-skated back and forth in the street as though they were ducks in a shooting gallery. Jenny was dancing nude on top of the third *O* on the Hollywood sign. And Eddy Price was swimming toward the bizarre scene through a sea of paperwork.

A ringing phone saved me from the bizarre perils of my dreams. It was my wake-up call. I showered, dressed, and then drove back to Sausalito, arriving at a cozy hiding place directly across from the Smith houseboat around 6:15. I kept the radio and my pipe going as I waited for Bernstein to show up. The pipe was going strong, as usual with my Tropical Mix, and the radio was offering the Eagles, Steely Dan, and an occasional new wave band thumping a headache rhythm into my ears.

I was letting my pipe bowl cool and had switched to the news when Bernstein drove up at exactly 7:00 P.M.

Helen Smith opened the door. Bernstein stepped in and shut the door behind him. He stayed inside during the sports and the weather and a tune from Blondie, then he and Helen Smith emerged and got into Bernstein's car.

They drove away and I followed at a discreet distance. As we drove across the Golden Gate Bridge my adrenaline was beginning to dance jazz routines through my body. I took a different toll booth than Bernstein did as we exited on the San Francisco side, and picked up the car again as we resumed our route toward downtown San Francisco. I missed a light Bernstein ran at about Geary and Seventeenth, but luckily traffic was heavy and I caught up with them two blocks later. We crawled our way to the heart of downtown, and Bernstein eventually pulled up in front of the Hyatt Regency. I coasted by and parked about a block past the valet parking. It was a red zone, but what the hell. If I got a ticket I'd just charge it to St. John.

By the time I got on the escalator Bernstein and Mrs. Smith were a level above me. They were involved in an intense, serious discussion and didn't seem to be looking for a tail.

They hit the lobby and didn't bother with the desk. Whomever they were going to see, they knew the room number. The Hyatt Regency was like something out of a *Star Wars* special effects lab. The lobby area itself was open to the roof, which was about seventeen stories up. All the rooms' main doors opened onto the vast open lobby. I'm afraid of heights and even looking *up* made my knees weak. The elevators looked like black wrought-iron teardrops. They were open, faced the lobby, ran up and down on chains, and looked far too precarious for an intelligent person to use. But they were usually full. People even came by just to ride in them.

I watched Bernstein and Smith ascent in one of the elevators and followed them visually to a door on which they knocked and through which they were granted entrance. Quickly I took the elevator to the same floor and walked past the door, noting the number, 1245. I didn't see a house phone on the floor so I went back down to the lobby and the front desk.

"Excuse me," I said to the woman behind the desk. "Could you tell me who is in room 1245?"

"I'm sorry, sir, but I can't do that."

I smiled at her, she smiled at me. We were both nice people. I didn't want the name for any underhanded purpose, of course, and she didn't want to refuse me. It was just company policy.

"All right, then," I said, still smiling. "Could you give me the room number of Kathy St. John?"

The woman looked through her book. Then she looked up at me and said, "Aren't you the clever one. She's in room 1245."

I told her thanks and raced for the elevator. I missed one that had just left. I got the next one and pressed 12.

It seemed like a day and a half before I reached the twelfth floor. I walked as fast as I could to room 1245 without running down the hall. I wasn't sure what I was going to say, but I was sure it would come to me. At least I'd found Kathy. That in itself was worth something. I could have made it to the room faster but I almost sprained my arm patting myself on the back.

I knocked on the door. No answer. I knocked again. Still no answer. I listened. No sound.

I tried to figure out how I could get somebody with the hotel to open the door, and still not leave the door unguarded. After all, I didn't want Kathy to escape. I was thinking this as I looked out upon the lobby. Then I saw them. Bernstein, Helen Smith, and Kathy St. John were going down an escalator on their way out of the hotel.

"Shhhit!" I said aloud. I felt like springing over the railing and landing on them. If I screamed at them, they would disappear, maybe for good. I raced to the elevator and waited long enough to read *Gone With the Wind* to a deaf person before the lift came. By the time I hit the floor, ran down the escalator, and out to the street, I could see the trio getting into Bernstein's car and driving away. I ran to my car, disgustedly plucked the ticket from its windshield, and sped off down the same street I'd seen Bernstein's car take. But it was hopeless. They had been swallowed up by the city and I was left with nothing to eat but a parking ticket and the thought that I might not be as good a detective as I thought I was.

I drove over to a little bar I'd noticed near my hotel and ordered a drink. The Stolichnaya soothed my bruised ego as I sat slumped in a corner booth trying to sort things out.

First of all, Kathy St. John was alive. She seemed to be going with Bernstein and Mrs. Smith of her own free will. She didn't even seem to be hiding, since she had registered at the hotel under her own name; that was a point in Everett Gray's favor. In fact, Gray's whole story jibed with what I'd seen.

And what in the hell did Bernstein and Helen Smith have in common with Kathy St. John? Obviously, Edward Smith had died while in the company of Kathy St. John and took a slug trying to get to a meeting with her. But what was so important? Whatever it was, it involved Bernstein and Helen Smith. Edward had to be the link. Another Stolichnaya, and the whole mess became a little more clouded. Another, and I was satisfied with the matter's sufficient clarity . . . at least until morning.

Simon Bernstein's San Francisco office waiting room reminded me of his office in Century City in L.A. His receptionist even looked like a clone of his receptionist down there.

"I'd like to see Mr. Bernstein. Is he in?" Actually I already knew the answer. I'd checked the building garage downstairs and his car, the one I'd seen him drive two nights in a row, sat in a space that had his name painted on it.

"Who shall I say wishes to see him?" asked the clone.

"Does he materialize or disappear on the strength of a wish?"

"What did you say your name was, sir?"

"I didn't, but the name's Carpenter."

"First or last name, sir?"

"Both."

"Carpenter Carpenter?" piped the clone.

"No. Just one name for both. Like Charo or Donovan. Look, just tell him 1245 Hyatt Regency. He'll see me."

"Just a moment, sir. I'll ring his secretary and see if he's in. Just have a seat."

I didn't have to wait long. He was in. His secretary opened a door to the reception room and led me to Bernstein's office. She showed me into the room and closed the door behind her as she left. Behind his desk Bernstein was puffing away at a pungent pipe tobacco.

"Mr. Carpenter, good to see you again." He didn't get up.

"Yeah, I'll bet."

"Sit down, make yourself comfortable."

I sat down, but I wasn't comfortable.

"I saw you, Kathy, and Helen Smith leave the hotel last night."

"I see," he said, puffing a little unevenly on his briar.

"I want to know what's going on."

"I don't understand," Bernstein said as innocently as a cat purring with feathers in his mouth.

"I think you do."

"Let me see if I do. Is Kathy wanted for some crime? Is she being legally sought on state or federal warrants?"

"No. But we thought she'd been kidnapped."

"You saw her yourself last night leave the hotel of her own free will. She was registered, alone, under her own name. Do you really believe she's been kidnapped?"

"No."

"Is Helen Smith wanted by the authorities?"

"No."

"Am I?"

"No."

"Then how can you come in here and threaten me with the information that three law-abiding citizens, one being myself, were observed walking out of a hotel together last night? Hardly a stiff charge."

"Do you deny it?"

"Why should I?"

"Do you?"

"You said you saw us, Mr. Carpenter."

"In other words, I'll have to prove it if I want it to stick."

"Mr. Carpenter, I thought you had something of importance to tell me. Apparently you do not."

"Bernstein, I'm on to something. You can help. If you don't, and criminal proceedings result, you might get mud on your face."

"I appreciate your concern for my appearance, but I assure you I know how to take care of myself."

"You know where Kathy is?"

"No."

"I called the Hyatt this morning. She'd checked out. If you see her, tell her that her father would like to hear from her."

"If by some coincidence I run into Kathy St. John, I'll give her your message."

I didn't bother to say thanks. I left the office thinking that Bernstein reminded me of someone. Then it hit me. He sounded just like David St. John. They were both lawyers . . . and both cold human beings.

I went directly from Bernstein's to Sausalito to see Helen Smith. All the way over I was trying to think of any leverage I had. Bernstein was a tough guy. Most lawyers were. They knew the law. Which was just another way of saying they knew what they could get away with without getting nailed. Most people didn't. I didn't.

I arrived at the Smith houseboat just before noon. There were a bunch of kids, most in their late teens, being supervised by an older man.

"Hi," I said to the man.

"Good afternoon, sir. What can I do for you?" he asked cheerfully.

"I'm looking for Mrs. Smith. I'm a friend of Simon's," I lied.

"Simon Bernstein?"

"Yes. As a matter of fact we just had a late breakfast near his office downtown. I'm a client of his from L.A."

"Jed Cleary," said the man, extending his hand.

"Tom Carson," I said, accepting his hand and shaking it. "So where is Mrs. Smith?"

"I'm surprised Simon didn't tell you."

"Well," I said, hedging, "he didn't send me over. In fact, we didn't even talk about Mrs. Smith. It's just that he's talked so much about her before, and what with Edward's untimely death and all, I thought I would stop by and pay my respects. You understand, Mr. Cleary, I'm sure."

"Of course. Edward's death was a blow to us all. We over at the center have felt a sense of disorientation since we heard. But we're coming back together. Edward always said that survivors use the momentum of adversity to their advantage. We're survivors, Mr. Carson. Edward Smith has helped us to be that way."

"And Mrs. Smith?" I said, serving as a rudder, guiding the conversation back on course.

"Mrs. Smith left this morning. To get away for a while. It's been very difficult for her here the past week."

"Naturally. Did she say where she was going?"

"No. But she'll be gone for some time—a month or two at least. That's what we're doing here—making things secure while she's gone."

"Did she drive, fly, or take a train out of San Francisco?"

"You seem very interested in Mrs. Smith, Mr. Carson," said Cleary suspiciously.

"It's just that if she's still available somewhere in the city, I'd like an opportunity to speak with her. You see, I met her husband in L.A. just before his death and, well . . . he said something to me that I think she'd find comforting."

"I see," he said, scratching his head. "But I think you're out of luck. Phillip took Mrs. Smith to the airport early this morning."

"Phillip? Is he around?"

"He's inside washing windows."

"Where?"

Cleary pointed to a young man in blue jeans and a yellow t-shirt.

I didn't wait to get Cleary's permission. I thanked him and moved past him over to Phillip.

"Phillip?"

"Yeah?" said the youth, stopping his work.

"I understand you drove Mrs. Smith to the airport this morning."

He looked at me and cast his face in a suspicious mold.

"I've just talked with Mr. Cleary and he said it was OK to talk with you. I'm a friend of Simon Bernstein. I met Mr. Smith just before he was killed. I wanted to contact Mrs. Smith because Edward said something to me before he died that I think she should hear." It was almost a sacrilegious lie and I wouldn't have told it again if I weren't desperate.

That seemed to melt Phillip somewhat.

"So you took Mrs. Smith to the airport this morning?"

"Yeah."

"Was she alone?"

"No. I drove her and a young woman to the airport."

"What did the other woman look like?"

He then proceeded to give me an exact description of Kathy St. John.

"Do you know where they were headed?"

"Yeah. I checked their bags with the skycap. They were going to L.A."

"You're sure?"

"Positive."

"Did they say anything else in the car that would give you an indication of where in L.A. they were headed?"

"No. They were pretty quiet. They whispered a lot, like they didn't want me to hear what they were talking about. They both sat in the backseat."

"OK. What airline did they take?"

"PSA. The 10:00 A.M. flight."

"Were they traveling light?"

"Two bags each. Looked like they were planning to be gone awhile."

"OK. Thanks. You've been a great help. I believe I know where Helen has gone. I'll catch up with her there." I shook the young man's hand and waved goodbye to Cleary, who, I could tell, in another minute or two was ready to be protective.

I had gotten real close. But just as it was with horseshoes and sex, close didn't count. In fact, being close often just left you feeling more frustrated. I'd lied to Phillip. I didn't have the slightest idea where Helen and Kathy were off to. For all I knew, they were just stopping off in L.A. to take an international flight to Sri Lanka.

I went back downtown, checked out of my hotel, and drove my rental car to the airport, where I deposited it and paid for its use. I bought a ticket back to L.A. And all I had to show were a few more curious facts and a couple of teased hunches.

I got back to L.A. about 5:00 P.M. and went directly to the West L.A. station. I'd called Eddy while I was waiting at the San Francisco airport and had run down the situation to him.

I got to the station about 6:30, collected him, and decided on Mirabelle's.

"So what's new?" said Spike as we sat down in a booth near the bar. He was wiping a glass. I liked to give Spike my business. He always watched the detective shows on TV and we would talk about what a bunch of crap they were—except for *The Rockford Files,* of course. In fact, James Garner had come into the bar one night while Spike and I were discussing the PI business from the early days of Pinkerton to the modern-day computer-oriented security biz. We'd both made fools of ourselves sending drinks to the table at which Garner sat with another guy. We finally went over to him and told him how much we liked the show, his acting, and his camera commercials. Fortunately, he was enough of a gentleman not to tell us both what a couple of putzes we were for bothering him.

"Oh, a few things," I said, and held up two fingers. That meant I was buying and that Eddy was having a Stolichnaya with me; at least the first round.

"How's tricks, Sergeant?" asked Spike as he personally came around the bar to deliver the drinks.

"Same old shit, buddy," said Eddy, claiming his drink.

"Know what ya mean, know what ya mean," moaned Spike, as if repeating a litany. But I guessed that Spike *did* know what Eddy meant. Spike left us and resumed his duty of dosing out sufficient quantities of liquid fuel to fire the warmed-over dreams of his regular Hollywood patrons.

"So you actually saw Kathy St. John?" Eddy asked,

taking his first sip of the Russian vodka.

"Yep. No doubt about it."

"And she wasn't under duress? Nobody's captive?"

"No way. At least that's the way it looked to me. And I don't think Bernstein's the kind of guy to get mixed up in a kidnapping. Bernstein's one cold son-of-a-bitch, but he's not stupid."

"I phoned St. John with your news . . ."

"Damn! Eddy, I wanted to tell St. John myself and see his reaction to certain things I say."

"Don't worry, I just told him you saw her. I told him I didn't know where or under what conditions, but that you were coming back tonight and would be in touch. I just told him Kathy was alive and apparently well."

"What'd he say to that?"

"He seemed relieved. Then he acted a little angry."

"How so?" I said, taking out my pipe and lighting it.

"Well, he said something like, 'Sounds like a stunt my daughter would pull.' I got the impression she'd done things like this before. Any idea where she is now?"

"I'd check her apartment, Josh's boat. I can check with her friend Penny and tell her to let me know if she hears from her. But, as I said on the phone, L.A. might just be a layover for Mrs. Smith and Kathy; they might be headed somewhere else. And what can we do if we find them, anyhow?"

"Helen Smith's not wanted for anything and, from what I've found out recently about St. John's clout around here, I'd better have one hell of a good reason to detain Kathy. I could ask her a few questions about Smith's murder, but besides that, she's free to go.

"Oh, by the way, you're probably off St. John's payroll by now. You found Kathy and she's OK. It's not part of your job to patch up family quarrels."

"Yeah, you're probably right. But I just can't help feeling as though there are a lot of loose ends just hanging there to be tied up. Dammit!"

"I have some news."

"If it's good, I'm all ears."

"Might be. We've got a line on Smith's assassin."

"No kidding," I said, coming alive, puffing a little harder.

"Yeah. We put a tail on St. John's exhouseboy and he led us to a guy named Robert Wong. Wong's brother, Benny, owns some martial arts place on the east side. Benny was a fighter at one time and did OK. Now he works freelance. Anyhow, he's supposed to be pretty good. And he drives a black Trans-Am. We got a picture of Benny to the dishwasher over at the Kavkaz and got a positive ID."

"Great. So what's the problem?"

"Benny's become a mole and we can't get him to show his face. We put some heavy pressure on Yamaguchi and the kid's scared as hell, but his lawyer's put a cork in his mouth. We need Wong."

"So how do you get Wong?"

"He's supposedly hiding out in Chinatown, waiting for some false papers and a way out of town. Those things can be arranged down there."

"I know. I've done a little business there myself."

"Any leads, you just pass them along, OK?"

"Sure, Eddy, you know me," I said innocently.

"I do. That's why I reminded you. In case you forgot, I'm the cop, not you."

"How could I forget, Eddy? You're the guy who gets me all those passes to the ballgame."

"I could also get you a pass to jail for a few days if your memory starts to go."

I raised my glass in his direction and suggested he buy the next round. He did. Only this time we drank beers: domestic and from the tap.

"You be careful when you see St. John tonight," said Eddy. "He's probably the kind of guy who kills people he doesn't like."

It was a comment he didn't have to make. The thought had already occurred to me more than once.

I called Penny from Mirabelle's, but she said she hadn't heard from Kathy. I told her to call me the minute she did. She promised to do that. We shot the breeze for a minute or two: I told her I hadn't read the book she'd lent me; she told me she was thinking about getting a dog and calling it Pluto.

Then I called my service and the only message I had was from a finance company asking if I needed to borrow any more money to pay my already overdue monthly payment. Those people are so damned considerate. Then I called St. John and told him I was on my way over.

He seemed more calm than I'd ever seen him. He was wearing a burgundy smoking jacket and slippers over silk pajama pants. A gold chain with a handsome piece of jade dangling from it hung around his neck. He was drinking something clear and offered me the same. I took a Stolichnaya and we sat down in his living room.

"I understand you saw my daughter," he said simply when we both had settled in and sipped a little.

"At the Hyatt Regency in San Francisco."

The name of the city made his eyelids dance, but he recovered nicely. I'd decided to play things fairly low-key with David St. John for the moment. The clues had led me to some interesting conclusions, but I needed hard cold facts, as well as the police to back me up before I cornered this big shot. Chances are he'd killed Smith, or had him killed, and the finger was pointing firmly in his direction as Jamison's murderer. Who shot at Kathy St. John still had me a little snowed, but her father couldn't be ruled out at this point. Without anyone to back me up, I'd be a free shot on goal for St. John.

"Why didn't you bring her back with you?"

"She wasn't alone. Nor, in my opinion, was she acting under anyone's will but her own."

"I see," he said, sipping at his drink. "And did you get a good look at the person or persons she was with?"

"I did." I knew the names were going to send his facial features to the races just trying to control his surprise, so I unloaded the words full blast.

"She was with Simon Bernstein and ... Helen Smith."

He started to say something, but only air came out of his mouth. He pressed his lips together tightly, got up from his seat, walked to the window, and stared out absently at the sprawling city with its million lights seemingly blinking off and on in the distance. I had the feeling St. John was looking even further than the thirty or so miles I could see, to a different place and a different time. As strange as it may sound, I got the distinct impression St. John was on the verge of tears. He looked like a man in dire need of someone to talk to. I wasn't that someone, though. I had to do something to bring him back to present time.

"What do you make of your daughter with an old friend of yours, and the wife of a man you never met, whose husband died trying to reach your daughter?"

St. John coughed a little, swirled his drink around the sides of his glass, swallowed hard enough for me to hear, turned from the window, and returned to his seat directly across from me.

"Very strange, Mr. Carpenter. I don't know what to make of it."

"I think you have more clues than you're willing to give me," I said firmly. The tone of my voice brought into focus my now rather demanding presence.

He looked as though he was going to deny my accusation perfunctorily, then raised his eyebrows in acquiescence. "Perhaps you're right. But that still does not mean I'm going to tell you. You work for *me*."

"But I found your daughter, did my job. I deserve some answers."

"You deserve nothing, Mr. Carpenter," said St. John, as calmly and inoffensively as anyone could have made such a statement.

"I'm not going to be the only one asking for answers."

"That may be true. It may not be. Regardless of that, I'm entitled to my privacy. As far as you are concerned, your duties are completed—rather well I might add. And your fee and bonus will reflect my appreciation of your professionalism." He stressed the last word. "Mr. Carpenter, do you know what I mean by professionalism?"

"Doing a job and nothing more," I said sardonically.

"That's close. I pay for professionalism," he said, which, translated, meant that if I decided not to make any more waves, I'd make a few extra bucks.

St. John's employer-talking-to-slave demeanor changed and he rolled his glass uncomfortably in his hands as he spoke. "So you saw my daughter with Simon and Mrs. Smith. Do you know where they took . . .where my daughter went with them?"

"No. I lost them. If you really want to know, call Simon Bernstein. The information I have is that Kathy and Mrs. Smith took a plane here to L. A. this morning. They could be in L.A. or just about anywhere else in the world by now."

"Did you get a good look at Mrs. Smith?"

"Yes. She seemed not to be holding up too well under the obvious strain of her husband's murder. You know, the thing I can't figure out is why Smith made contact with your daughter in the first place."

"Neither can I, I assure you."

"Is it possible that your daughter was having an affair with Edward Smith?" I didn't really think so, but I just wanted to see St. John's eyebrows dance again. They went into whirling dervish motions.

"My God, no! That is totally out of the question. She and this young man . . ."

"Bill Jamison."

"Yes, Jamison, were having an affair and I've never known my daughter to date anyone older than thirty. By the way, that's too bad about the Jamison boy."

"You needn't express remorse. You told me yourself he was a punk."

"I was not expressing . . . remorse, as you say, but rather stating the obvious. It is too bad that he met the end he did and that Everett Gray seems to be innocent of the crime. Because that makes me a prime suspect and so far I have not been able to come up with anyone to back up my alibi. Jamison's murder was committed at a time when most people are home in their beds asleep. And since I usually sleep alone, I have no one to corroborate my story. As you can see, I stay informed."

"I hear you're connected downtown like a rivet to iron."

"I have influence, but I do my best not to abuse it."

I noted that he didn't say he *didn't* abuse it, just that he did his best not to. Hitler could have said he did his best to try and like Jews. He didn't do such a good job. But he could have said he tried.

"You don't seem very worried about Kathy, if I may say so," I said, lightly rattling my cubes in the bottom of my empty glass. He didn't take the cue.

"Mr. Carpenter, my daughter has obviously seen fit to take an excusion incommunicado, as she has done many times in the past. Unlike the times in the past, a murder and her own near-miss with death convinced me that this time was different, more serious, that she may have met with foul play. That does not seem to be the case. Thus, I'm relieved, yet somewhat disappointed in my daughter's lack of concern for my feelings. As far as your being her bodyguard is concerned, I don't think she needs one now, and if she does, I'll not pay one to follow her all over the world. From here on in, if she wants my help, I'm at her disposal. But I'll be damned if I'll beg her to let me help her."

After I'd heard the speech and came to grips with the fact that St. John wasn't going to fill my glass again, I decided to call it a night.

"Look, it's been a long day. I'll call you tomorrow and see what's going on."

"Mr. Carpenter, I don't think you understand. Our relationship is over. I hired you to do a job. It's done, and that's that. I have your address and phone number and I will send you a check tomorrow. If I should require your services again—and that I doubt—I will call you. Do you take my meaning?"

"I can read between the lines," I said. "Basically, my employment is terminated."

"Not basically. Essentially, irrevocably, completely."

We played word games for a few more minutes and then he showed me out.

As I walked down the long asphalt driveway to my car, I could tell from the light reflecting down the path that St. John was still standing at his door. Watching. It gave me a funny feeling. I had good reason to believe that St. John was a murderer. Being watched in silence on a dark night by someone you think is a killer can give you a strange feeling. He was still watching me by the time I got into my car and headed back down into the city, where other killers were watching other victims.

* * *

I called Jenny and she was home. She asked me over.

She was just what I needed now. Besides, I wanted to ask her for a favor.

She met me at the door wearing a Danskin top and heavy stockings that came up to her thighs. Her hair was pulled back off her face, which looked like a porcelain China doll's face. She wore nothing under her burgundy leotard and the outline of her nipples could be seen as well as a seductive outline of the little mound between her legs.

She threw her arms around me and wrapped her legs around my waist. She was light and her warmth felt good. I carried her over to the couch and we both sat down.

"Oh, honey," she said, kissing me tenderly on my lips, "I couldn't sleep last night worrying about you. I had a bad dream the night before that something had happened to you. I called your place and I couldn't get a hold of you."

I let her show her affection for another few minutes, then she fixed me a drink and sat down, legs curled up underneath her, facing me on the couch. I told her about San Francisco, even about the nude wrestlers. She thought that was kind of kinky and was on the edge of her seat during my description of my near-meeting with Kathy St. John at the Hyatt Regency.

Then I told her about Benny Wong and that he was hiding out in Chinatown.

"Jenny, I think you can do me a favor."

"Anything," she said, more than a little playfully.

"You told me once that you had a very good friend who was in touch with the shadier sides of Chinatown."

"That's right."

"You think he might be willing—as long as it doesn't put him in a tough spot, of course—to give me some information as to how to find Benny Wong?"

Jenny raised her eyes to the ceiling looking at something I couldn't see. She considered my proposal for a few minutes, then a little smile spread over her face. "I think I can get the information, but . . ."

I was afraid I knew what her condition was, but I let her state it. "Yes?"

"You've got to let me go with you."

"Are you kidding!" I half-laughed.

"Absolutely not. That's my condition."

I took a gulp of my drink and stared into the glass. I knew Jenny. She was an avid detective book reader and envied anyone who did the work. Also, she could be incredibly stubborn. So stubborn, in fact, that there was a definite possibility that she *could* help, but might decide not to if her terms were not met. She uncurled one of her legs, stretched it out straight, and ran her long fingers sensuously up the calf to her thigh and stopped just short of home base. She was a hard negotiator.

"OK," I said. "But only to a point."

"What point might that be?" she asked, replacing her leg into a more ladylike position.

"You can come along with me until I figure you're in danger."

"Do you mean if lead starts flying?"

"I wouldn't put it in that cliched a terminology, but basically, yes."

"You've got a deal. When do you want me to call my friend?"

"Now."

"Now?" she smiled and uncurled both her legs this time. She meant business.

It didn't turn out to actually be "now," but it wasn't long afterward, as we were lying in bed, that she made the call. My orgasm had been like the white from a nuclear explosion and I was still working my way back to reality through the fallout when I heard her say, "Thanks, David, we'll go right down."

As I gradually came to, I saw Jenny putting on a pair

of straight-legged jeans, black high-heeled shoes, and a
tweed jacket over a pink t-shirt, which had a picture of
Woody Allen on it. She tossed my clothes on the bed
and went to prepare us each a megadose of liquid caf-
feine.

Over coffee she explained that David, her friend, *had*
heard that Benny Wong was laying low in a warehouse
on Broadway on the outskirts of Chinatown. He had put
her on hold while he'd made a couple of calls. Benny
Wong wasn't well-liked by David. Although an under-
world figure himself, his money was always "clean."
That is, nothing from drugs or prostitution; he was in
business and proud that his word meant something, as
did the word of his associates. Benny Wong was not a
man of integrity, according to David. He was a thief, a
hothead, a liar, and, the mortal sin, had recently tried to
make inroads into "local business interests"—a fact that
had been of great concern and consternation to David
and his associates. Yes, David knew where Benny was
and David and his associates had made it clear that Benny was no longer welcome in L.A.

David's family being friends with Jenny's family in
Singapore had led over the years to David taking a
fatherly interest in Jenny's well-being, while not trying
to run her life, nor reporting back to the family about
her lifestyle or questionable vocation. Since she would
not accept financial assistance from him, he had never
refused her any of the infrequent requests she had made.

After she'd told David why I wanted to know where
Wong was, he'd considered that it might be even better
to have Wong in jail—put there by me instead of him—
than run out of town. So, with Jenny's reassurances that
I would call the cops in as backup, he had given her the
address of the warehouse.

"What we need is a plan," said Jenny, peering over
her coffee cup at me with wide, excited eyes.

"I'm not going to let Eddy grab all the glory. I'll move

in first and by that time Eddy should be on the scene."

"I don't think that's a good idea. You're not Wyatt Earp."

Certainly that was a simple, reasonable enough observation, but the purport of it hadn't really impressed itself upon me as much as it should have. I thought about it and let it sink in.

"Yeah, you're right." I got up, went to the phone, and called Eddy. I made him promise to at least let me in on the capture in return for the info. Reluctantly, he agreed. Eddy told me to meet him at the corner of Broadway and Sunset and that we'd move in from there.

On the drive over to the rendezvous point Jenny was electrified with excitement. We covered and recovered all the possible situations and dangers of the plot we had so suddenly set in motion. We were going after a killer, Jenny and me, and we both agreed that we now knew how Nick and Nora must have felt.

I spotted Eddy and a blue-suit sitting in their pea-green unmarked car in a bank parking lot at the corner of Sunset and Broadway and pulled up next to them. I got out and walked over to the car. He rolled down the window.

"So what's the plan, chief?" I asked.

"Follow me over to the warehouse. That's 'follow' as in do what I say; no improvising."

Not exactly Webster's, but I got the message.

"I've already got about six black and whites surfounding the warehouse. And," he continued, cocking his head in the direction of my VW, "what in the hell is Jenny doing here?"

I explained the terms of my deal with her. He wasn't impressed. "Don't worry, Eddy. I'll make her stay in the car."

"That's nice. You sure she shouldn't just go in first to see if it's safe for us guys?"

"Look, I couldn't have gotten the information any other way."

"OK, OK, stop whining," he said, shaking off the argument that was eating into precious time.

I returned to my car and told Jenny Eddy's rules. She had thoughts about putting up a fight, but realized that it wouldn't do any good.

"Stay in the car, OK? Eddy can come down on me so hard, you could carry me around in your wallet afterward. If things don't go right in there, his ass is on the line and he might need a scapegoat. Don't give him any reason to nominate me."

"All right," she said, only mildly deflated. After all, she would still be as much in the thick of it as the officers on the periphery surrounding the warehouse.

"One thing, though," she said, touching my arm as I shifted gears.

"Yeah?"

"Be careful. This is exciting and the danger is stimulating, but this is not a movie. Don't get hurt, Ace. I'd like to do it all again sometime." I waited for the director to yell cut, but all I heard were traffic noises in Chinatown.

What could I say? Naturally I said that I would be careful and that there was nothing to worry about—that Eddy was actually in charge and I was just along for the ride. She knew what I'd say, but it made her feel better to hear me say it.

We pulled into the parking lot in front of the warehouse behind Eddy, and I got out and walked around to the passenger side. I retrieved my .38 from underneath a false bottom in my glove compartment and stuck it in my shoulder holster. Eddy was met as he was getting out of his car by a uniformed officer. I kissed Jenny on the cheek and left her to join Eddy. The uniformed officer was telling Eddy that everyone was in place, all the exits were covered, and that no sign of Benny Wong, or anyone, for that matter, had been observed.

"You, Ramirez, and you, Johnson," said Eddy, pointing to two uniformed cops standing by their black and white about twenty feet away. "Come with me."

Then Eddy took me by the shoulder and whispered so that no one else could overhear him. "Ace, you're a shadow. I don't want to hear you, or have you be in the way, you got that?"

"You're the boss," I said, nodding obediently. I could tell that Eddy was nervous. He knew about Benny Wong —that the guy would kill us if he got the chance. That kind of knowledge can make anyone feel a little uneasy.

He turned back and signaled for Johnson, a black, and Ramirez, a Chicano, both of whom had shotguns, to follow him. I tagged along. The three had their guns drawn and I patted my shoulder holster just to make sure I could make a good impression if someone asked me to play show and tell. It's funny how cold steel can make you feel so warm.

Eddy had already received permission to search the warehouse from the owner, who had supplied the police with a key.

We all went around to the side door and Eddy tried the handle. It was locked. He used the key and unlocked the door.

We all got into crouching positions and, one by one, ran into the dark warehouse to our first position.

The place was immense and piled high with boxes, crates, and opened merchandise consisting of television sets and stereo equipment.

There were two aisles down the width of the warehouse, and one large aisle that ran down its length, separating it into equal halves.

"Ramirez, you and Johnson go that way; take the left side," said Eddy in a whisper, pointing to our left with his gun, "and we'll take the right aisle. When you get to the center aisle, stop and look to your right for us. We'll acknowledge each other with one wave. If anything's wrong, wave twice, back and forth, like this," said Eddy, demonstrating. "We'll do the same."

Ramirez and Johnson took off down the left aisle and Eddy and I started down the first. It was a great place to hide, I had to say. A man, or even a couple of men could easily conceal themselves behind or inside a box and never be found. I took a deep breath as I watched Eddy stalking about twenty feet in front of me. We walked in silence and the only sound I could hear was my heart pumping blood fiercely to my head. My mouth was as dry as a church on Sunday.

Suddenly I heard a sound directly to my left. I whipped my gun around in that direction and a cardboard box flap tapped lightly against the side of a box, animated by the slight breeze coming in from an air circulation system directly over it.

I tried to swallow, but it was like gulping a glass of dust.

Eddy had arrived at the center aisle, which divided the place in two. I joined him. Johnson and Ramirez were both standing about thirty yards to our left as they had already reached the center aisle themselves. Johnson waved once, Eddy did the same. Then we all crossed the center aisle and continued our sleuthing mime. By the time we got to the end of the second half of our row I was ready to celebrate another birthday, or so it seemed.

When I reached Eddy at the end of the aisle, he appeared worried. I looked to my left for Johnson and Ramirez and didn't see either one. Eddy and I waited another thirty seconds or so and finally Johnson appeared. He waved once. Then again.

"Shit!" said Eddy in as loud a whisper as he could say it. "Wong's got Ramirez. Ace, hustle your ass outside and get some help in here. Now!"

He didn't have to invite me twice to leave. I turned and ran down to the center aisle and looked both ways.

No sign of Ramirez or Wong. I ran down the other half of the aisle and just before I reached the end I heard a door open. A bright light came flooding through the warehouse to where I stood. I could see Wong's back. He had a gun to Ramirez' head. I had great compassion for Ramirez, but I also felt a little sorry for Wong. Things aren't always the way you see them on TV. Cops can get pretty pissed off, even for little things. But you put a gun to the head of a fellow officer and even if you gave up, threw down your gun, and crawled into the squad car, you had just bought yourself a world of hurt. By this time Eddy and Johnson had joined me and we were all watching the drama unfold.

"I'm coming through. Bring me an unmarked car. Now!" Wong shouted. "You assholes better move or your buddy's a dead man. Move!"

Just then I heard some tires screech and a pea-green Chevrolet was delivered to Wong. The driver, a cop, got out and faded back into the light. It was amazing how quickly he'd gotten the car. I'd have to remember the ploy the next time I wanted a cab in New York. I'd just take out my gun, grab the doorman, and make my demand. But then, in New York people were too used to seeing other people with guns to their heads.

Quickly Wong and Ramirez disappeared into the car.

"If I see a black and white or an unmarked cop car in my mirror, I'll kill this guy," shouted Wong through the open car window. "And don't forget, I can monitor your calls on the police radio. Don't be more stupid than you already have been."

With that eloquent commendation, Wong sped away. Johnson, Eddy, and I raced out the door. I ran past the chaos to Jenny, who was sitting in the car. The look in her eyes was something between numb fear and exhilaration.

"I'm going after Wong. These guys can't."

"I'm going, too," she said. I didn't have time to argue.

I whipped my VW around—as much as a VW can be whipped around—and headed out onto Broadway toward downtown. I could see the car about two and a half blocks ahead of me. It seemed to me that by this time Wong should have had a longer lead. I followed the Chevrolet at a length of about a block and a half down Broadway until Wong pulled into a parking lot at the corner of Broadway and Third. I cruised slowly on past. As I did I saw Wong standing beside the car and kicking the back left tire. Obviously some shrewd cop had thought quickly enough to cut a tire on the car. The left rear tire was now totally flat. I stopped the car a block beyond Broadway and Third and got out.

"Call headquarters and tell them where Ramirez and Wong are, and that I'm going after Wong. Hurry!"

"But Ace . . ."

"Hurry!" I ordered and shut the door. I ran a half block back down the street. I then slowed to a normal walk as I neared the parking lot where I'd seen Wong and Ramirez. I took a deep breath. My heart was beating like a drum in a marching band as I got to the parking lot. The driver's side door was open, but Wong was nowhere in sight. I carefully approached the car. Ramirez was inside, slumped over in the front seat. I got in and checked for any signs of life in the abandoned cop. His heart was beating, but he had a nasty gash just above his left eye.

I looked around again for Wong. There was only one entrance to any building from the parking lot, and it led into the Bradbury Building. I went to the side entrance . . . the door was unlocked. I walked in and listened. I was in a dark hallway that led into a well-lit lobby. I heard footsteps. Besides that sound, the building was asleep. I'd been in the Bradbury Building before. It was built about a hundred years ago and its marble staircases, open, black wrought-iron elevators, skyroof, and potted palms combined to serve as a time machine in downtown L.A. transporting the visitor back to the days when Marlowe himself was on the case.

I heard moaning in the darkness to my left. As my eyes adjusted I saw a security guard lying on his back. I went to him and checked him over. He'd be all right, but not for a little while.

Footsteps were coming from my right. I moved out into the lobby and there on my right, walking along the open second-floor balcony, was Benny Wong. He turned and looked around for signs of anyone following him. I ducked out of sight. As he passed between one of the spotlights that lit the balconies and a long hallway, Wong cast a long shadow, which revealed an extension in his right hand. It looked like a puppet on his fingers. And I knew Wong could make it sing and dance. But that was a show I'd pass on if I could. He was walking away from me and I climbed the stairs like a character in a silent movie. When I reached the top of the second landing Wong was about fifty feet in front of me. He turned to his left and walked down what I knew to be a short hallway. As soon as he disappeared from view I quickly covered the distance between the second floor landing and the entrance to the hall. I flattened myself against a wall that stood at a right angle to the hall Wong was in. I heard his footsteps stop at the end of the hall. Then there was silence. Apparently Wong had not known he was walking into a cul de sac. I heard the sound of footsteps again. They were getting nearer. In a few seconds Benny Wong would pass, armed, within five feet of me. There was no turning back. If I didn't take him, he'd take me. The footsteps got closer. I hadn't shot my gun in a long time. But I still knew how to use it. It's just that I hated to, because whenever I did, somebody got hurt.

Suddenly the sound of footsteps had a picture to go along with them.

"Hold it, Wong! Drop the gun!"

Wong reacted as though he'd just sat down on a paper spindle. He whirled around and started to point his gun at me. I squeezed off two shots, and Wong went down. I raced to the fallen man, kicked his gun out of reach, and surveyed the damage. After all, I wanted Wong to talk. I'd hit him in the shoulder and the arm. He was in pain as I held my gun on him.

There was a big commotion downstairs and I heard Eddy's voice. "Ace! Ace!"

"It's over, Eddy. Come on up. Wong's down and I've got him covered."

Eddy and about twenty uniformed officers appeared, guns drawn, and secured the area. I put my gun back in my pocket and did a fade-out into the parking lot, where Jenny's anxious, welcoming arms, as well as other essential warm body parts, were waiting to give the hero his just reward.

About four hours later Eddy called me at home and told me to meet him at Theodore's. It was important and it would be a stopover on our way to St. John's. Jenny and I were getting settled in by that time, but I got the distinct impression from Eddy that the payoff was at hand, and I'd already invested too many quarters not to be around.

Eddy'd already ordered beers by the time I arrived, and he was chewing on a pretzel from a brown plastic bowl which almost decorated our table.

"Wong spilled his guts," said Eddy after I'd sat down.

"I imagine after a little coaxing he was ready to tell you just about anything, including his prenatal experiences."

"He was willing to tell us that, but we didn't ask."

"How's he doing?"

"He's still breathing."

"So what did he say?"

"The nuts and bolts of it are that St. John's houseboy, Yamaguchi, made contact with Wong at a bar in Chinatown. Yamaguchi gave Wong five thousand dollars to kill Edward Smith, with the promise of another five thousand when the job was completed. The second payment was made at the Golden Lilly, also in Chinatown, the day after Smith died. We've been in touch with Yamaguchi and his lawyer, and Yamaguchi's gonna serve us St. John on a platter. In fact, I've got a warrant for St. John's arrest right here in my pocket. I thought you might enjoy being in on the pop. After all, you helped more than a little."

"Thanks, Eddy."

"Besides, I have the feeling he'll do a little talking. He's a lawyer—he'll know what to say and what not to say. It might be interesting."

We downed our brews, paid our tabs, and I followed Eddy up to Blue Jay Way to knock St. John off his roost.

Two black and whites waited outside while Eddy and I walked up to St. John's door to deliver the bad news. St. John didn't look too startled when he answered the door. I figured one of his friends had heard about the warrant and alerted him.

"Come in," he said, and we did. St. John was wearing a silk robe over black pajamas with red piping.

Eddy read St. John his rights and St. John nodded.

"Be seated, gentlemen," was St. John's calm reply. I took out my pipe paraphernalia and lit a bowl of Tropical Mix as Eddy and I sat down.

"I admit to the obvious paying of money to Wong, through Yamaguchi, but you are wrong about Jamison," said St. John simply. "I understand that the evidence looks bad, but it's all circumstantial and, to be blunt, you haven't got a shred of real evidence."

No one wanted to take credit for Jamison's murder.

Gray had turned down the privilege and now St. John was passing it up. But then, a murder rap wasn't the kind of prize people lined up to collect.

"There will undoubtedly be some jurors who will not look that harshly upon what I have done," said St. John coolly.

"Committing murder might be a real attention getter, but it doesn't win points in popularity," I said.

"That's true. But then, it wasn't too long ago that a man who found his wife in bed with another man could be successfully defended."

I didn't totally understand, but I had the feeling that my vague hunch was now going to be validated.

"This *is* Hollywood, but leave the theatrics to the actors. Just give us the facts," said Eddy in his best Sergeant Friday.

St. John, who was still standing, walked over to the large window that looked out upon the city. It was the same window he had stood at and basically the same view he had observed during my last visit. Again he seemed to be looking at someplace faraway. This time he took Eddy and me there.

"A little over ten years ago," he began, "my wife and I and Kathy"—it was the first time I remembered hearing St. John say his daughter's name—"were living in Pasadena. I won't pretend that we were the perfect all-American family, but I personally was happy. My wife was the most social of persons, while I enjoyed relaxing and being surrounded by simple domestic tranquility after finishing the business day. But our lifestyle ended up being a compromise; I never completely won any argument with Ellen, my wife.

"In the late sixties, as I'm sure both of you gentlemen will remember, many women were caught up in a certain kind of antifeminine militancy. The word domestic became simply another word for boring and 'un-hip.' My wife was nothing if not 'with it.' She decided to start back to college. She had had only a year's higher education before Kathy was born. Upon returning to UCLA her major became psychology, a subject that I don't mind saying bores me to death; especially when preached by a novice fascinated with what he or she considers to be ultimate insights into the psyche of mankind.

"I don't know how much you found out about my wife, but although she was loyal to me, sexually, she was not above a discreet affair now and then—this, too, was encouraged by the 'new-found spirit of freedom' among the fairer sex."

As far as I could tell, St. John had a "short-end-of-the-stick" point of view of the women's movement, but, like most stereotypes, it contained grains of truth. However, sometimes you had to look hard to find them.

"While attending UCLA in the summer of 1968 my wife became involved with a teacher's assistant named Edward Montigue. When the affair had gone on for more than three months, I confronted my wife with information I had collected. She pleaded for my forgiveness and promised to end the affair. To make a long story short, she resumed her affair with this man. When I confronted her with new information, she laughed at me and brashly told me that that was just my tough luck.

"Though it might be difficult for you gentlemen to understand, given that I allowed my wife to conduct her 'clandestine activities,' I am a proud man. Cuckolding me and subsequently flaunting it in my face was too much for me to bear.

"Every winter Ellen, Kathy, and I would go to Zurich for a vacation. Naturally, that particular winter I was in no mood for a family vacation. I sent Kathy to vacation with my parents in Colorado, while I stayed home, telling Ellen that I didn't care what she did. I found out that she was planning to take our Zurich vacation herself, but not alone. As you must know, Ellen and her family are quite wealthy, so Ellen arranged the Zurich holiday for herself and her lover, Edward Montigue.

"When I found out her plans I was blind with rage. But I am a methodical man. Therefore, I formulated a strategy for revenge. I tell you what I am about to tell you now for two reasons. First, it will come out soon anyway, and second, I have already admitted to the murder of Edward Smith. But strangely, as you will soon understand, I was under the impression I had already had him murdered ten years ago."

Eddy and I exchanged looks. St. John was still staring out the window when Eddy looked across at me and said, "Holy shit!"

"You see, I paid an assassin to kill Edward Montigue and dispose of his body by putting it into a car and pushing the car off a cliff to a fiery grave, burning the body beyond recognition, and beyond the ability of authorities to discover that there had been foul play. In retrospect—and I have been going over this in my mind for many days—my mistake was telling my then best friend, Simon Bernstein, of my plan. Because Simon, though my closest friend, was also my wife's friend and himself an incredibly ethical individual. He told me in so many words that he was terminating our friendship—although he would not turn me into the police—because he could not be the friend of a man who had other people murdered.

"He must have alerted my wife and Montigue. Just how they avoided my hired assassin, I don't know. You'll have to ask my wife, who I'm certain you have deduced by now is still alive and the widow of Edward Smith, also known as Edward Montigue."

Eddy and I looked at each other again. This time Eddy's eyes said holy shit! That was the connection I had sensed all along, but couldn't put my finger on.

"My wife's feigned death must certainly have been

easily arranged. Money can buy anything, gentlemen. Anything," said St. John, with a certainty that sent chills down my spine.

"She obviously paid her guide enough money to support the tragic story of her death. As you will recall, her body was never recovered. And so she and Edward Montigue have been free to live under their new identities since then. A complete erasure of their old identities worked out perfectly for both of them. It was evident that I would opt to have Edward killed rather than grant a divorce. I found out that Montigue himself was married and his official death served as a no-strings ticket out of his marriage, which, of course, was failing as badly as Ellen's and mine."

"But why now after all these years did you have him killed?" asked Eddy, as much out of fascination with the story as to gain evidence.

"Simple. The information just recently came to me. Edward Montigue has become more visible recently, even with his beard to hide his face, and that was his undoing."

"You shot or had Montigue/Smith shot on his way to meet with your daughter."

"That's right."

"Did she know that her mother was still alive?"

"To the best of my knowledge, I don't believe she did. I have not been the ideal father to Kathy, but I have done my best to be both mother and father. Her mother abandoned her ten years ago. Abandoned!" repeated St. John with a strain in his voice that indicated to me that St. John still felt the pain of being abandoned himself.

"Why, after ten years, then, did Montigue try to contact Kathy?"

"You'll have to ask Kathy that question."

I noticed he didn't say he didn't know, he just said that we'd have to get the answer from Kathy. It seemed obvious that Montigue/Smith had contacted Kathy with the intention of letting her in on the family secret.

That much was clear from the fact that I'd gotten Ellen's phone number from Kathy's notepad next to her bed. But what the hell made it so urgent now? Urgent enough for Montigue/Smith to risk his life and spend his last living moments trying to accomplish it.

"But I did not kill Jamison. And that's the truth," said St. John, turning and facing us.

I don't know why I was ready to take the word of a confessed murderer, but I believed him. It was a strange feeling. I'd just listened to St. John tell us that he had paid to have a man killed, but I had to admit I had compassion for the guy. It was the first time he'd revealed a human side of himself to me. Maybe it was the first time he'd revealed that side of himself, a side with which he was very familiar, to anyone. It was out in the open now. He seemed to look relieved. But it was hard to tell whether it was all over for St. John, or just beginning.

Yet something still bothered me as Eddy led St. John away and we all headed back down the hill. Why now? What or who was the catalyst. Then it hit me. I knew who the catalyst had been. And it fit. The whole damn thing was falling together at last.

Even though it was now about 5:00 A.M. there was still a light on at Maureen Style's when Eddy and I drove up in front of her house on La Jolla. I told Eddy I thought it was all right if we went in by ourselves. He agreed but stationed a black and white in the alley by the back door and another remained out front near Eddy's car.

I knocked on the door. A startled, tough-looking Maureen, dressed in a heavy floor-length robe and leather moccasins, opened her door the length of a chain and peered through. "What in the hell do you want?" she barked at me.

"Police," said Eddy, flipping open his ID, revealing a badge.

"I don't have to . . ." she began to argue.

"It's all over, Ms. Montigue," I said. That turned her off as abruptly as lifting a needle from a blaring phonograph record. There was silence. She shut the door, unchained the lock, and let us in. Eddy and I sat down on a dilapidated couch and Maureen took a chair opposite us. "How'd you know?" she asked me. There was a look in her eyes I'd not seen in them before. Gone was the harshness, the brass. A deep wound had been exposed and she was bleeding before our eyes.

"I wasn't positive, but a few things seemed to add up. I talked with a girl you used to work with and she mentioned that you always had your slaves wear an ID bracelet with the initials E. M. on it. No one involved with the case had those initials and, to be honest, it didn't seem that important when I first heard it. The most important clue revolved around a sense of urgency in Edward Montigue/Smith's wanting to reach Kathy St. John. No one close to him noticed anything drastic happen to him except for one thing—your argument with him. For some reason that no one close to Edward could explain, you greatly upset a man known for his calm. And no one knew you or what you'd said. At first, in fact, until just recently, I had you pegged for a blackmailer, but I never came across any glue to make it stick.

"And St. John, who has just admitted having Edward murdered, gave a pretty lame excuse as to why he just recently decided to have Edward killed. But I think I know why he chose to do it now."

Maureen looked blankly at me.

"You told St. John you'd found the man who'd run off with his wife, didn't you?"

She took a deep breath. She had only the most fleeting thought of arguing. She had reached the end of a long road on a journey that had begun ten painful years before.

She took a cigarette from a pack sitting on the arm of her chair, lit it, and exhaled the smoke.

"Yeah, I told St. John. I never really believed that my old man had been killed in Switzerland. Even though I was only about eleven at the time, I knew what was going on with my folks. My old man, the great healer of minds, used to beat up my mother in front of me. Nice, huh. I'll spare you the gory details. To make a long story short, I saw a picture on the back of one of 'Edward Smith's' books, and I recognized the eyes. It was the eyes that hit me first. I took away the beard and the longer hair and realized it *could* be my old man. But he used to weigh a lot more. I wasn't sure. I'm his daughter and I still wasn't sure until I'd talked with him for a few minutes.

"So, I went to see him at his center over on Sunset the night before he was shot. I confronted him with my accusations. At first he tried to deny them, but then he admitted they were true and he got real cold. I threatened to go to David St. John with what I knew—I'd known about the woman my father went to Zurich with because my mother finally told me when she figured they were both dead.

"My threat sent Edward over the edge. His whole 'new' life would be ruined and his respectability destroyed. Then he started calling me names. He said I was just like my mother, a no-good, alcoholic slut. He told me he'd started running around with other women because he'd found out my mother had tricked him into getting married by saying she was pregnant. Back in '58 that kind of thing still happened," said Maureen, crushing out her cigarette in an ashtray on the coffee table in front of her.

"He said he'd married my mother 'to do the right thing,' but that she'd been made pregnant by some other guy she'd been running around with. The child, of course, was me. He said she didn't tell him he wasn't the father until one night five years later when she was drunk and had spent the night with the same guy, who'd come back in town for a few days.

"After that, he said, he couldn't stand the sight of me for a long time, but gradually he came to tolerate my presence. Tolerate my presence," she repeated, her voice cracking a little on the last word.

"To her dying day my mother loved Edward. I spent nine years in hell with my mother after my father deserted us to go away and live the high life in Europe with Ellen St. John. My mother died last year of alcoholism, and I held her hand nearly every night for those nine years and heard the same story over and over about how Edward Montigue had left his family for another woman. I did that instead of my homework all through junior and senior high school. I didn't go to college. I went to work . . . as you both know.

"My father's story might've been true, but that night I wouldn't have believed it if he could've shown me films of what went down. All I could hear was the voice of my dead mother drowning in her pain, dragging me down with her, calling my father's name. More than anything in the world I wanted to hurt him as badly as I'd been hurt.

"Then Edward said something that drove me crazy. He said, 'Pull yourself together. Have some class. Be an adult. Look at Ellen's daughter. She had to go through the same pain you did and she's come out of it all right.' My mind just flashed red and I stormed out of the center. What the hell did he know about my pain? He had no idea. Kathy St. John was a rich kid with a rich father. She didn't suffer the way I did. My mother died in my arms because of what my father had done, and my life was ruined. While Kathy St. John took trips around the world—I read about them in the newspaper—I put flowers on my mother's grave. Edward killed my mother as sure as if he'd put a bullet through her head. And he had the nerve to stand there and tell me that my life had been as unscathed as Kathy St. John's.

"I know it isn't logical, but I came home immediately, called my slave, Stanley, commanded him to come over, then ordered him to take his gun and shoot Kathy St. John. Even if she didn't die, I was determined that she would feel some pain. Feel some of my pain, dammit!" cried Maureen.

"I'd be damned if my mother and I were the only ones who were destroyed by what happened. Then I called David St. John and told him about Edward."

"So that's why St. John finally decided to act," I said. "It was the first moment he *knew* Edward and Ellen were actually alive."

Eddy took down the name and address of Maureen's slave and dispatched a black and white to pick him up.

It was all a pretty good night's work, and I was just about out on my feet. There were a couple key questions yet to be answered, but my mind was beyond even asking them. I headed over to Jenny's, and Eddy went home. We'd agreed to meet at the Palms Restaurant for a 10:00 A.M. breakfast and make a fresh plan to tie up the loose ends.

"I still don't understand exactly why Edward Smith contacted Kathy St. John," said Eddy, sipping coffee and pushing a yellowed plate of half-finished soft eggs to the side of the table.

"I think there's only one person who can answer that question now and that's Kathy St. John. She knows what Smith said to her on the phone that night after he'd talked with Maureen at the center, why Smith gave her Ellen's phone number—which, by the way, is a pretty good indication that Kathy didn't know her mother was alive before that night. And finally, only Kathy knows what Edward said to her in the limo before he died."

"But where in the hell is Kathy St. John?" asked Eddy rhetorically.

"The answer to that question, buddy, would win us all

the prizes. But let's not forget there's another murder here nobody wants to sign his or her name to—Jamison's. Gray's story seems straight and matches Jamison's neighbor's version of the story. The number one suspect after Gray is St. John and he doesn't have a good alibi. If he did it, I think he'd have set up one hell of a solid one. And Maureen and her henchman didn't have a reason in the world to kill Jamison."

"Somebody had one."

I followed Eddy back to the station, where a message was waiting for him. Everett Gray urgently wanted to see him; he had important information regarding the Jamison murder.

About thirty minutes later Eddy and I were sitting in a visitors' room at the jail waiting to see Gray. He was brought into the room by a guard, who left when he saw Eddy. Gray sat down across from us at a long wooden conference table. Eddy offered him a cigarette. He took it and a book of matches from Eddy, lit the cigarette, and tossed the matches back across the table. He was dressed in blue-gray prison clothes, but he seemed in relatively good spirits.

"Let's start at the beginning, shall we? I met William Jamison about a year ago at the Coastal Cruiser, where he was a waiter, and we became . . . good friends."

"You became lovers?" I asked.

"William was a little down on his luck and, well . . . I showed my appreciation—as most lovers do straight or gay—in a way that William found helpful. William made money as what you might call a gigolo, servicing some of the older women—and men—in Santa Monica, Malibu, and the Marina. But he was nickel and diming his way to nowhere.

"One thing led to another and I became quite fond of William and wanted to help him in a big way; something to get him the kind of freedom a young man like William deserves. He had a very difficult childhood, you know. But anyway, I told William about a sweet little setup I knew about that could make him some real money. And with his way with women, it was a golden opportunity he just couldn't pass up."

"And what setup was that?"

"David St. John isn't Kathy's real father."

I stared straight ahead as though Gray had just recited the weather report, but what he'd said hit me like a ton of bricks.

"And you know who her real father is?" asked Eddy.

"No doubt about it. Ellen St. John's longtime lover before she married David St. John and for a few years after is the same guy who's taken a 'fatherly' interest in Kathy all her life."

"Josh Wade," I said.

"You got it. William was blackmailing Josh Wade. William threatened to tell David St. John that Josh was Kathy's real father. And, as you know, David can be the violent type."

"And you've sat on this for twenty years?"

"Writing about Society people, one must be discreet. Besides, although David St. John and I didn't see eye to eye, Ellen and I were very close. I was a confidante for her. And I would never in a million years think of doing anything to hurt Ellen. She was dead, anyhow.

"But Ellen's alive," I said.

"But you must remember I didn't know that until Kathy told William that on her way to San Francisco to see her mother."

"Why didn't you tell us Kathy was going to see her mother?"

"I felt that I'd betrayed Ellen's trust by turning William on to her daughter. I was close to Ellen, not to Kathy, so I guess it didn't bother me too much when I thought Ellen was dead. But when I found out Ellen was alive, I had an attack of conscience. I wanted to keep her out of this as much as possible. Besides, at the time, I thought I could beat the murder rap. After all, I didn't kill William. But I've been talking with my lawyer and he tells me that David St. John is a prime suspect in William's murder. And, since neither of us has any good alibi, I'm the most likely to take the fall if the real killer isn't caught. I don't have to tell you how much influence David St. John has. He got me fired once. He doesn't like me very much."

"So your attack of conscience was turned back by an attack of self-preservation."

"You might say that."

"I did," said Eddy.

"Before Edward died in the limousine, he told Kathy her mother was still alive. Then, after Smith died, she went to William's house and told him that she was going to go see her mother in San Francisco to hear what she had to say. She told William that she wasn't going to let *anyone,* especially her father, know where she was going, and that William shouldn't worry. That's when William got the idea to hit St. John up for twenty-five grand. He knew that Kathy wouldn't contact David St. John for at least a few days, which would be time enough to take the money and run. Poor, poor, sweet William.

"The news that Ellen was alive came as a shock to me, and I urged William to put a stop to blackmailing Josh Wade, which had been going on for about four months. He'd already gotten to Wade for about five thousand dollars."

"That makes Wade our next stop," said Eddy.

"And unless I miss my guess, we'd better make it fast," I said, already getting up from my chair and making for the door.

There were four black and whites waiting by the time Eddy and I arrived at the Marina pier. One of the officers reported to Eddy that they'd been watching the boat for the past fifteen minutes and had seen no sign of anyone on board. We approached the *Last Resort* and stopped when we reached its side.

"Josh Wade!" called Eddy into the wind. It was only about 11:30 A.M., but the sun was hot. A gentle breeze from the ocean helped to cool things off, though. The setting was calm, quiet—the kind of quiet that gets you thinking about heading for cover.

I heard a door slam inside the boat and Wade appeared on deck, wearing a gray sweater, white slacks, canvas shoes, and a yellow scarf around his neck. I recalled the day he'd lied to me about who he was yelling at on the phone. It figured that Jamison had been the other party. Just what Jamison had threatened him with was now pretty clear. My guess was that it was the same threat—exposure to St. John—but the asking price had just gone sky-high. Jamison was getting ready to make the big play and split.

"What can I do for you, gentlemen?" asked Wade. It wasn't a cordial greeting. He said it as though he knew exactly what he could do for us.

"We'd like to ask you a few questions," said Eddy, taking out his badge and showing it to Wade.

"Yeah," said Wade resignedly and waved us aboard. Eddy and I stepped on board in full view of about ten uniformed police officers thirty feet or so down the pier. Wade motioned for us to be seated in deck chairs. We sat down and Wade leaned against the boat railing.

Eddy informed Wade of his rights and then primed the conversational pump. "Let's not beat around the bush. We know a lot, we just need you to fill in the blanks. We know that Kathy St. John is your daughter, that Helen Smith is Ellen St. John, Kathy's mother, and that Bill Jamison was blackmailing you."

Wade became a cloud in the otherwise sunny day. If he could, I think he would have started to rain. I always had a certain sympathy for people who offed black-mailers. Such scum just took and took and destroyed peoples lives, moving otherwise normal people into the only act that could free them of the parasite. Wade looked like a man who'd been dancing on broken glass. He was in pain. He closed his eyes, gently slapped a hand to his forehead, and pulled it down over his face and chin, opening his eyes again to see if it was all just a bad dream that'd go away.

But the bad dream spoke again. "Mr. Wade, would you care to make a statement?"

"What do you want me to say?"

"I want to know if you killed Bill Jamison." said Eddy simply.

Wade sighed deeply, shut his eyes, inhaled again, and, without opening his eyes until after speaking, said, "Yes."

Wade looked at each of us, searching for some compassion. In Eddy's face he saw none. In mine, he did, so he directed his monologue toward me.

"It was too much. I just couldn't take it anymore. I'd already given him more than five thousand dollars. His last demand was for thirty thousand dollars and that would not have been the end of it with a person like Jamison, I assure you.

"If David St. John had ever found out about Ellen and me, he would have had me killed, just as he did Edward."

"We know about that," said Eddy.

Wade's face displayed minimal surprise.

"How long have you known about Ellen's being alive?" asked Eddy.

"Nearly all along. I've been keeping an eye on our daughter as much as I could over the years. Kathy's such a good girl; she deserves more," he said to no one.

"Do you know where Ellen and Kathy are now?" I asked.

He got an uneasy look on his face as he shook his head.

"There's no need to lie anymore," said a feminine voice coming from the stairway leading down to the cabins. We all turned to see Ellen St. John Smith standing with her arm around her daughter, Kathy. Behind them I could see Simon Bernstein and Billy Wade. The foursome joined us on deck and Bernstein made the first comment. "I've advised all the parties of their rights and I reserve the right to instruct them whether or not to answer your questions. Against my advice, Ellen wishes to make a statement."

Eddy filled her in on what we already knew so we could all make it home for dinner. Ellen St. John Smith looked like a sick woman. Though she must have been only in her forties, she looked to be older; her skin color was almost gray. To me it looked as though she was wearing a wig. She looked pallid, undernourished. She sat down in the deck chair next to mine. Billy Wade stood proudly next to her husband, and looked to be supporting his weight more than a little. Simon and Kathy stood behind Ellen's chair as the older woman talked.

"Whether I am a good or a bad mother is not at all in question here. The fact is, I have been a complete failure as a mother and I admit it. Three months ago I was told that I have less than two years to live. It was at that time that Edward and I started talking about my seeing Kathy once more. Not to try to make up for my leaving her or to set things right, but simply to say that I was sorry and to see if anything could begin from that point forward. Edward and I knew that contacting Kathy would be a tricky business, as is evidenced by Edward's death. The simplest plan we could think of was to make contact with Kathy through Josh, who has never revealed that I was still alive, nor that he was Kathy's real father. But something exploded our plan to bits last week. Our timetable had us contacting Kathy in the next few weeks when Josh would bring Kathy up to Sausalito on this boat. But when Maureen confronted Edward, she threatened to tell David everything. It would not be out of the question for David to kill Edward *and* me, or, at the very least, to send Kathy away from me to some distant, unknown place. And I don't have the time to waste tracking her down.

"After Maureen talked with Edward, he called me and told me what was going on. He told me that he'd contacted Kathy and told her only his name and asked her to meet him at a restaurant the next afternoon. He gave her my number to call in case anything happened to him and he didn't show for the meeting. But he made her promise not to use the number until either he talked with her, or didn't make the meeting.

"The day after Edward was shot, he picked Kathy up at the hospital and told her the basic facts of the story and pleaded with her just to see me. Not to forgive me —or him—for what we'd done to her life, but just to meet me, to let me see my daughter once before I die. Funny how things change, how priorities rearrange themselves when you know you're going to die. But then, everybody knows they're going to die. I guess we just try really hard to forget. After I learned that I didn't have long to live, only two things mattered to me: Edward and Kathy. And I'd given one up for the other. Edward understood how important it was for me to have my one last chance with Kathy, and gave his life so that I could have it. Now that I've seen my daughter and talked with her, touched her hair, looked into her eyes, seen her tears—through my own—I cannot even recall, as hard as I try, what in God's name could have made me leave her. Whatever it was, it is no longer a part of me. It's too early yet to tell what will happen with Kathy and me, but I know that I feel much more at peace."

I looked at Kathy. She looked as though the jury was still out on how she felt about the mother who had deserted her to go off and live with another man. But then, at least she had one parent who really cared about her, which was probably one more than she had ever had before.

"I have a question," said Eddy, when Ellen had finished. "Whose body was substituted for Edward Montigue's in the car crash that David St. John set up in Switzerland?"

"Money can buy almost anything," said Ellen. "I contacted the man my husband paid to kill Edward. The man procured a cadaver from a local medical school and sent it over the cliff in Edward's car."

"Mr. Bernstein," I said, "what really went on at the meeting you had with David St. John at the California Club the night Edward Smith was shot?"

"I called David on Edward's behalf. Edward knew that David must have hired the man who shot him. He sent me to tell David that if he didn't back off we would take the information about David hiring an assassin to kill Edward in Switzerland to the police. We still have the name of the man David hired. This time David didn't have time to try to make Edward's death look like an accident. He knew that since Edward knew that David knew, Edward would act quickly to defend himself, or maybe try to take Kathy to meet her mother."

"Why didn't you go to the police with the incriminating evidence against David St. John after Edward died?"

"If the papers got hold of the facts of this case, Ellen's name would be smeared across the country, as well as bringing inadvertent and unfair disgrace to Kathy, who is totally innocent. Time is more important now to Ellen than justice. Naturally, I didn't tell David that Ellen is dying, so he didn't know I was bluffing when I said I'd go to the police. If Kathy is willing, Ellen would like to spend her remaining time with her. A trial of this magnitude could quite possibly outlast Ellen's life. And even if it didn't, Ellen and Kathy could never be allowed the privacy and intimacy they may need in the coming year."

"What about all the money Jamison had?" asked Eddy, turning his attention again to Josh Wade.

"It's down below in my cabin."

"Including David St. John's twenty-five thousand dollars?"

"I suppose so. It was just a suitcase full of money. I didn't count it. I just took the suitcase and ran."

As I looked at the silent members of the party sitting and standing on deck, the interrelationships seemed to blur together. And so did right and wrong.

I called Jenny from Mirabelle's and gave her enough information about the day's adventure to whet her appetite and told her I'd be by in about an hour. Then I proceeded to tell Spike the whole story. He loved every word and whenever anyone ordered a drink, he treated that person as though he or she were imposing. He was quite nearly in awe of me, a working private eye. I didn't often wilt people in swells of admiration, so I played the part for all it was worth: about five Stolichnayas, to be exact.

"So what's gonna happen to St. John?" asked the bartender.

"Don't know. He'll see the inside for a little while, but probably not long enough to miss a dry cleaning pickup, or an important awards banquet. Same with Wade. Bernstein's a good lawyer, and Wade's never been in trouble before. It doesn't take Rembrandt to paint Jamison as a pretty bad guy."

"What about Kathy and her mother?"

"You got me. I hope they can work it out. Kathy seems like she's been waiting a long time for somebody to say, 'I love you' and mean it. For all her faults—and they're many—Ellen St. John looks like she really means it."

"It's a damned shame ya gotta push people up against the wall before they know they got something to lose," said Spike.

"Yep." I nodded. "The world moves pretty fast these days and the old values seem to have gotten lost in the shuffle. And the only time they reappear is when you take the initiative to slow down or life slows *you* down. Not many people have much control over their own lives these days," I said, downing what I vowed would be my last drink . . . before Jenny's.

"Not you, though, Ace. You're about the only guy I know who's got control, who's doing what he wants to do. You wanta be a PI and, by God, that's just what the hell you are," said Spike, lifting a glass and toasting me.

"Damned right," I said, a little tipsily.

"It's a hell of a gamble trying to live a life doing what you want to do, and that's a fact," said Spike, setting his glass down.

I nodded absently, got up off the bar stool, turned to leave, then stopped. I turned back to Spike and said, "Nope. The gamble is trying to live a life *not* doing what you want to do."

Spike blinked and thought about that a minute. Then he smiled. He understood.

So did I. At least for the moment. As I walked out onto Sunset with its cars, bright lights, and empty promises flashing like a pinball machine gone haywire, I was hoping I'd remember it tomorrow.